BATTLE KING

PRINCES OF DEVIL'S CREEK BOOK FOUR

JILLIAN FROST

BATTLE KING

PRINCES OF DEVIL'S CREEK BOOK FOUR

JILLIAN FROST

Also by Jillian Frost

Princes of Devil's Creek

Cruel Princes

Vicious Queen

Savage Knights

Battle King

Boardwalk Mafia

Boardwalk Kings

Boardwalk Queen

Boardwalk Reign

Devil's Creek Standalone Novels

The Darkest Prince

Wicked Union

For a complete list of books, visit JillianFrost.com.

BATTLE KING

PRINCES OF DEVIL'S CREEK BOOK FOUR

JILLIAN FROST

PART ONE

THE BATTLE KING

Chapter One

LUCA

I must have killed the right criminal to deserve this life. There was no other explanation for why I was lucky enough to call Alex my wife. She was perfect, everything I ever wanted.

Thanks to Giovanni Angeli, we had the entire beach to ourselves. The Sicilian Mafia boss arranged for us to have one last day where no one would bother us. Not even tourists were allowed to step foot anywhere near this place. His men had set up a perimeter that forced people to drive in the opposite direction.

I sat on the blanket beside Marcello, watching Alex come for Bash. Her eyes flicked between us as she rode my brother into the sand, her blond curls bouncing on her big tits. Damian was on the other side, rubbing his hand over her sweet ass.

We fucking loved her.

Worshiped her.

There wasn't anything we wouldn't have done for our queen.

Alex was seven months pregnant and technically not allowed to travel overseas. Not with her C-section planned for the end of the month. But we needed an escape, so I coordinated with doctors in Italy just in case she went into labor.

Out of breath from coming so hard, Alex put one hand over her heart, the other on her baby bump that seemed to grow every day.

When my phone rang, she glanced at me with one eyebrow raised. "Luca."

I held up my hand. "I know, baby."

I promised no calls.

We'd almost made it one week without interruptions. I instructed the Knights not to disturb us unless it was a dire emergency. So when Sonny Cormac's name flashed across the screen, I had to take the call. He wouldn't have disobeyed my orders without cause.

Alex leaned over to look at the Caller ID. "It must be important. You should get it."

I put the phone on speaker so everyone could hear. "This better be good, Cormac."

"Drake is gone." Sonny struggled to catch his breath. "The Lucaya Group blew up his lab at Battle Industries."

Alex covered her mouth with her hand and gasped. "No."

We'd lied to Alex for the past month, telling her everything was okay. That Drake was safe. It was a precaution to keep her from panicking, which wasn't good for her or the twins.

"You need to get home," Sonny continued. "You're not safe."

Just like that, our honeymoon ended with the phone call I dreaded. I planned the trip to get Alex out of Devil's Creek. We hadn't had the opportunity to leave the country, not with multiple threats hitting us at every angle. My brothers agreed a vacation would be a good change of pace—something to take Alex's mind off all the darkness in our lives.

Until last year, we thought The Lucaya Group killed Bastian and Damian's parents. It was the lie Fitzy told to keep us from discovering his deception. The terrorist group had other reasons for attacking The Devil's Knights.

They wanted Drake Battle.

Drake developed artificial intelligence software that put him on the radar of tech giants, worldwide governments, and even crime syndicates. A powerful software that, in the wrong hands, could start a war.

People feared artificial intelligence and had every right to do so. That was the reason Drake canceled the program. The beta of Lovelace was too unstable to release into the world. Unfortunately, our enemies knew about it because of all the press.

Some people claimed Drake was a billionaire set on taking over the world. Others believed he was a genius, a pioneer ahead of his time. There was nothing like Drake's software on the market.

"Get home now," Sonny said into the receiver with panic in his tone. "The Knights need their leader." He paused for a moment. "There's one more thing… I found a girl in a Mac Corp shipping container. She's the daughter of Cian Doyle."

Marcello took the phone from my hand. "Are you fucking kidding me, Son?"

"Afraid not." Sonny groaned. "I left her at the safe house in Beacon Bay."

"Cian Doyle is Declan's enemy." I glanced at my brothers and shook my head. "Why the fuck haven't you handed her to him?"

Sonny was the nephew of an Irish Mob boss. Before his mother married into a founding family, she was one of the infamous O'Sheas. The Founders almost didn't allow Sonny's dad to marry her because of her connection to organized crime. But when you're as powerful as the Cormacs, the rules don't apply.

"Because I'm trying to figure out what she's hiding,"

Sonny said in his defense. "I'll deal with the girl. Don't worry about it."

"Get rid of her," I ordered. "Alex is ready to pop out the twins. We don't need another crazy mob boss breathing down our backs."

Alex wasn't handling this pregnancy as well as the last one. With Sofia, she was fine up until the delivery. The postpartum depression made it harder for her to bond with her daughter. And with the twins, she was having a lot of panic attacks. Her anxiety was getting out of control. Some mornings, she woke up unable to breathe until she realized it was a dream.

The four of us tried to shield Alex from the truth. She knew Drake and some of the Knights had attempts on their lives. To ease her concern, we worked from home.

It had been more than six months since I went into Manhattan, the headquarters of Salvatore Global. Same with Bastian and Damian. They were running Atlantic Airlines from the home office they shared. It was like all of us were on house arrest.

God forbid Marcello even thought about leaving for a mission with Alpha Command. Alex would throw a fit and beg him to stay. We chalked it up to pregnancy hormones.

"I'll handle it," Sonny assured me. "It won't blow back on any of you or the Knights."

"It better not," I said in a firm tone. "We'll leave tonight."

I ended the call.

Alex lowered the sundress over her head and fixed it over her baby bump. She looked beautiful, her skin tanned and glowing.

Standing in front of me, she bit the inside of her cheek. "Luca, should I be scared?"

"We'll get Drake back."

The words stung my tongue because they felt like a lie. I hated how much we had to conceal from Alex, but it was to keep her and the babies safe.

I hoped Drake could handle the interrogation long enough for us to rescue him. The Devil's Knights had to undergo extensive training during initiation. We had to endure hours or sometimes even days of torture.

Not for the faint of heart.

I stroked Alex's cheek with the pad of my thumb. "We'll find Drake."

She cocked an eyebrow at me. "Alive?"

I nodded. "That's the goal."

Alex smiled and grabbed each of our hands, ordering us to place them on her stomach. She ran her fingers over our skin as we stared at the water. "I wish we could stay here forever."

"Me too," we whispered in unison.

It was the truth.

If it were possible to live in Italy and never go back to Devil's Creek, I would have jumped at the chance. Alex was calmer while on vacation. I hadn't seen her look so at peace in a long time. The stress surrounding our family and the Knights was too much for her.

After one last look at the water, I drove toward Giovanni Angeli's compound with the top down on the convertible. Alex sat beside me with her curls blowing in her face, a smile gracing her pretty pink lips. My brothers were in the backseat.

Why couldn't we have gotten another hour with our wife before we had to return home?

Alex propped her elbow on the armrest, staring at me. "Are you okay?"

No.

"I'm fine. Just focused on driving."

I hated lying.

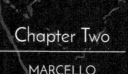

Chapter Two

MARCELLO

After we arrived at Giovanni Angeli's compound, I called Sonny. I needed to know how The Lucaya Group got to Drake. With all his gadgets, weapons, and security, he should have been impossible to reach without leaving a pile of bodies behind.

Sonny answered on the second ring. "Cello, hey."

My best friend was the only person who called me that and got away with it.

"Tell me everything you know about Drake's kidnapping."

"They took Drake on his way home from a demonstration for the Army," Sonny said, frustration dripping from his tone.

I shook my head. "How the fuck did they get to Drake with soldiers surrounding him?"

"They waited until Drake was twenty miles from the testing site before they ambushed his convoy. Tate Maxwell was with him."

"Shit." I sat down to get my bearings, tugging at the ends of my hair, and sand shook from it. "If they took Tate, they know he's important to Drake." I brushed out the rest of the sand with my fingers. "They're going to use him to get information from Drake."

Sonny exhaled loudly into the receiver. "Yeah, but Drake can handle interrogation."

"He won't sit there and watch them torture Tate." I held the phone to my ear and lowered my voice. "I'll go in with Alpha Command to get them. But I need time to access Drake's system to triangulate their location. Do you have any leads?"

"I don't know how to do that tech stuff." Sonny snickered. "Good thing Drake's been teaching you and Cole."

"I'll start working on an extraction plan with Alpha Command. But I can only do so much from here. Where's Cole?"

"He's at home. Grace just delivered Hale."

Not the best timing.

Hale was Cole's first child with his wife.

I couldn't imagine having to leave Alex hours after she delivered my son.

"Cole is ready to go and knows the risks," Sonny said. "He'll do whatever it takes to get Drake back."

Cole Marshall was Drake's cousin on his father's side and graduated from York Military Academy. He had the proper military training and started work at Battle industries last year. As an engineer, he had access to Drake's software and knew the ins and outs of his business.

He was the only person other than Tate Maxwell who knew enough about Lovelace and Drake's protocols. I hated asking him to come with me and Alpha Command, but it was necessary.

It was high risk, and for that reason, I couldn't tell Alex the truth. Instead, I had to act like it was a regular mission with Alpha Command. She would overreact and panic, putting herself back on bed rest. And with how high her heart rate and blood pressure had been throughout this pregnancy, I didn't want to upset her.

None of us did.

I sat on the closed toilet seat and leaned forward to rest my elbows on my thighs. "What about the container girl?"

He paused for a moment and then chuckled. "I don't know what to do with her. I could turn her over to my uncle Declan. But the girl seems innocent. I doubt she has any involvement in her father's businesses."

"She may be useful," I pointed out.

If Luca weren't preoccupied with the Drake situation, he would have used her to get something from her father.

"I'm keeping her in the apartment next to Damian's torture room."

I snickered at the thought. "I'm sure that place smells great."

"Hey, it's not the Ritz Carlton," Sonny tossed back with a chuckle. "But it will do until I find a better place for her. I can't take her home."

She wouldn't be welcome at the Cormac Compound. Sonny's mom was the sister of Declan O'Shea, a crime boss from Beacon Bay. Handing over this girl would have been a death sentence. And since we had a hard rule about hurting women or children, there was no way we would give her up without cause.

"What's her name?"

Sonny took a puff of his cigar. "Ella."

Ella Doyle.

Aiden spoke about her a few months ago. He ran into Ella at The River Styx, the bar in Beacon Bay owned by The Serpents. They got drunk and hooked up. But he hadn't mentioned her since.

"Ask Aiden to talk to her," I suggested.

"Why?"

"Because he knows her."

"Shit," Sonny grunted into the phone. "What's he doing with the enemy's daughter?"

"He didn't know who she was until after he fucked her."

A chair creaked in the background as Sonny spoke. "I don't think she knows anything. But it's suspicious that she ends up in a shipping container owned by my family. Don't you think?"

I rose from the toilet seat and stood in front of the mirror, pushing my messy black hair into place. Alex loved my wild, untamed look. Luca yelled at me throughout our childhood because of my unkempt appearance. He said I looked like a slob, like I didn't give a fuck—because I didn't.

"Whoever put Ella there knew someone from your family would find her."

"It's not just that," Sonny interjected, concern clouding his tone. "I found her in a container with guns for Declan."

"Well, that changes the game."

"Sure does," Sonny commented. "Whoever put her there did it with the intention of Declan finding her. They didn't know I checked each container before letting the owners go through the contents."

"I wonder what they were hoping to gain tossing her in there."

Sonny sighed. "I'm wondering if it's Killian Madden."

Killian Madden was as crazy as they came and ran a much smaller operation than Cian Doyle and Declan O'Shea. He was known for the cruelest and most unusual punishments. Even conversing with him was like stepping through a portal into another world. He was as crazy as the Mad Hatter and even made people solve riddles in exchange for his help.

So I could see somebody like Killian putting the girl in the container to fuck with Declan.

But why?

"What time was Drake ambushed?" I asked.

"Drake hit the emergency button on his watch around six thirty, I think."

"I need the exact time, Son."

"Six forty-eight Central Time."

"And what time did you find Cian's daughter?"

"Hold on. I have to go through the logs at the port." Sonny paused for a moment. "Seven forty-eight Eastern Time."

"So, the same moment you opened the container, they took Drake."

"Yeah, fuck." Sonny tapped what sounded like his fist onto a hard surface. "What do you think this means?"

"It's either a coincidence, which I doubt, or The Lucaya Group put that girl in the container to start a war. Find out what that girl is hiding. She's keeping something from you. The information might lead us to Drake."

"The threat of turning her over to Declan might scare her straight. I'll see what I can get out of her."

Luca opened the bathroom door and poked his head inside before entering. He moved beside me in front of the sink and placed his hand on my shoulder. "Are we good?"

I nodded. "Just getting a few details straight with Sonny."

"We leave in five," he said before exiting the room.

Chapter Three

ALEX

I stared out the airplane's window at the beautiful Italian coastal town. Calabria looked like something out of a magazine.

Picture perfect.

I sat between Luca and Bastian on the sofa with their hands on my thighs. Damian was across from us at the table with Marcello.

"We have to get Drake back," I whispered to no one in particular, wondering what I would do if someone captured my husbands.

Luca slipped his fingers between mine. "We'll find him, Drea. Don't worry about Drake. He's trained to withstand just about anything."

I snapped my head at him. "They're going to torture him until they get what they want. And then, they'll kill him."

"The Knights go through months of hell to become a member. Trust me, baby girl, Drake can handle it."

Marcello typed on his laptop, his fingers flying across the keys. He'd been on that thing from the moment we got on the plane. With Drake out of commission, Marcello was the only one who had the computer skills to track him. Thankfully,

Drake had been teaching Marcello for years. And my hubby was a good student.

"How did they blow up Drake's lab at Battle Industries?" I asked, still in disbelief over the situation. "Drake has more security at his headquarters than a military base."

"I don't know, baby." Luca ran his hand over my stomach. "Marcello is looking into it now. We should know something soon."

"I'm almost in," Marcello said with his eyes on the screen. "Drake activated Battle King protocol. So Lovelace locked everyone out of the system." He tapped his fingers on the table. "I'm just waiting for Cole to give me the authorization."

I leaned against Luca, and he wrapped his arm around me. "They took Drake and his head of security? Did they get anyone else?"

Marcello glanced at me. "No, just the two of them. But Drake is in good hands with Tate. He's a Marine and can handle himself. I wouldn't be surprised if they escape before we get to them."

My stomach twisted into knots at his words. "We?"

"I have to go after them, princess." His expression turned to stone as he focused on me. "I'm in charge of Alpha Command. I have to lead my team."

I could see right through him.

Marcello didn't want me to worry.

"What will you do with the girl Sonny found in the Mac Corp shipping container?"

Luca scrubbed a hand across his jaw, his pretty blue eyes aimed at me. "She's the daughter of Cian Doyle. That gives the Knights leverage over the Irish Mob."

"Sonny will find out what she's hiding," Marcello said as he went back to typing on the laptop. "The daughters of powerful men don't show up in shipping containers for no reason. Someone put her there on purpose."

"Finding Drake is our number one priority." Luca stuffed

his cell phone into his jacket pocket. "Then we'll worry about the Irish." His fingers brushed over my belly, something he did at least a hundred times a day. "Let us handle this, okay?"

I loved how much he took care of our babies and me. He was so sweet and loving, despite his cold exterior.

"What am I supposed to do? As the Queen of the Knights, I want to help Drake. He risked his life to get me back from the island. And he's always been there for me."

Luca's nose brushed my earlobe. "You have one job right now. Take care of Leonardo and Michelangelo. Too much stress isn't good for them."

While we were standing in the Sistine Chapel, staring at the world's most beautiful fresco, their names popped into my head.

Legends.

Creators.

Innovators.

Our boys would be just as legendary one day and needed strong names to carry on the Salvatore legacy. Besides, Luca wanted one of them to have the same initials as him.

Bastian inched his hand up my thigh, pushed up my dress, and nuzzled his face in the crook of my neck. "How about we finish what we started on the beach?"

"She needs a stress release," Damian commented. "Isn't that right, Pet?"

He leaned forward on the bench across from me, staring at me with his usual predatory gaze. And when he licked his blood-red lips, my insides melted like lava. Even after all this time, my husbands still sparked the same wicked desire inside me.

I lifted my sundress and gave him a little show. "Come play with me, Damian."

He slid off the bench and crawled over to me. My God, I loved when he was like this. It seemed crazy to me that I used to fear him. But that fear quickly turned to desire.

Before we left the villa in Calabria, I took a shower and didn't bother to put on panties. So I moved my hand between my thighs and touched myself for Damian.

Bastian leaned over and kissed my neck. "Are you teasing us, Cherry?" He shoved the curls off my shoulder and licked the length of my neck. "You taste so fucking good. I want to eat you."

Damian's eyes flicked between us as Bastian tortured me with his hot kisses. My sexy hunter gripped the backs of my thighs, looking up at me as he licked me straight down the center.

"Oh, God," I moaned, gripping a handful of his hair. "Damian."

All of my guys treated me like a queen and devoured me. But there was something special about Damian. Even Bastian agreed with me on that. Because whenever he put his mouth on us, we were both fucking dead.

Bastian stroked the hair on Damian's neck as he ate my pussy. Marcello stopped typing and grabbed himself over his pants.

"Make our wife cum," Luca ordered.

Of course, he was always in control. None of us ever complained because what was the point? Luca would always be a little bit of an asshole.

With my legs over Damian's shoulders, I leaned back and tugged his hair. He was so beautiful, perfect in every way.

I screamed his name and rode his face like a greedy bitch. His tongue felt so damn good I didn't want him to stop. But as I came down from my high, he sucked on my clit one last time, his lips glistening with my cum.

"Bedroom," I muttered, releasing my grip on Damian's hair. "Now. All of you." I raised my hand to beckon Marcello, who had his left hand on the keyboard. "You, too, husband. Take a break."

Marcello's face brightened with a smile that touched his

blue eyes. When I first moved into the house, he used to look so sad. Now, whenever I caught him looking at me, there was a softness around his eyes. He seemed at peace until today.

Our lives would never be simple.

My husbands promised we would always have to look over our shoulders. There would always be another enemy, another threat. It was the nature of the Knights' business, and as their queen, I had to slap on a smile. I had to pretend it wasn't killing me to lose one of my Knights.

What if I lost one of my men?

I couldn't bear it.

Chapter Four

ALEX

Luca and Bastian helped me up from the leather bench. My stomach was so damn big. It was like having my body invaded by aliens. These boys never seemed to sleep on my schedule and constantly bugged me.

Like their daddies.

When we entered the bedroom, tears dripped down my cheeks. Just the thought of raising the kids without my guys caused my heart to pound so hard it was ready to explode.

"It's going to be okay, princess. I promise." Marcello bent down and kissed my cheek. "Nothing is going to happen to Drake or me."

That was what worried me most.

Without Marcello, we weren't a family.

"I love you," he whispered. "We all do."

"I love you, too." I stood on my tippy toes and hooked my arms around his neck. "I don't want you to go."

"I won't be long. In and out, just like when Alpha Command helped us rescue you from the island."

"Come here, Cherry." Stripped down to a pair of black boxer briefs, Bastian patted the mattress. "We're hungry." He licked his lips, and so did Damian, who kneeled on the bed beside him, naked. "And we want a taste."

I flashed a sly grin. "Take off your boxers."

Luca undressed in the corner of the room, carefully laying his jacket and shirt over the chair. He was such a neat freak. But he needed order in his life to function.

I stripped off my sundress and got into bed with Bastian and Damian. On my knees between them, I tugged on the waistband of Bastian's boxer briefs. "What are these still doing on? Let me see that big dick I love so much."

Bastian inched the boxers over his hips, and his long length sprang free. He gave himself a few strokes, precum dripping from the tip. "Is this what you want, Cherry?"

I licked my lips. "Uh-huh."

I scooted closer and felt his smooth skin. Without hesitation, his lips crashed into mine, stealing my breath.

I peeled my lips from Bastian's, and then we kissed Damian. The three of our tongues tangled in harmony, locked into a passionate kiss that sent electric shocks down my arms.

Luca waited his turn on the bed to my right. He liked to have me to himself before I fucked the others. But, unlike my other husbands, Luca had a hard rule about double penetration. I could understand not wanting to do it with Marcello, but he could have at least caved with either Damian or Bastian.

He was a greedy motherfucker.

Luca flattened onto his back and snaked his arm around me. "Ride me, baby girl."

With Marcello's help, I climbed onto Luca and straddled his thighs. He didn't give me a second before pushing inside, filling me to the hilt.

"Luca," I whimpered.

He was so damn big.

I turned my head to the side to watch Damian flick his tongue over Bastian's bottom lip. With that, Bastian palmed the back of his head and kissed him like he was angry. Like a sexy devil trying to suck the soul from his body.

Every time they kissed, it was rough and aggressive. And so damn hot. I watched them growl into each other's mouths like hungry animals. Bastian curled his fingers around Damian's throat and groaned as Damian jerked his cock.

I could have stared at them all night.

Luca grunted as he made love to me, soft and slow. "You feel so good, my queen."

Marcello nibbled on my earlobe and massaged my left breast, the warmth from his breath heating my skin. "You're so beautiful, princess." He kissed my neck. "So fucking perfect."

Luca's fingers burrowed into my hips, his thrusts more aggressive. "Fuck me."

I wasn't as steady with my big stomach, so Marcello held onto me, helping me fuck his brother. They both worshiped me, each doing their part to make me feel like a queen.

Like their queen.

Luca took his time and made every second feel like I was floating above my body. Whenever I was pregnant, he was so gentle. I didn't see his rougher side until long after I had Sofia. And now that I was carrying his boys, he was even more loving.

He rocked into me, brushing his fingers over my belly. A rare smile graced his lips, and I returned his gesture.

With Marcello on his knees beside me, I reached over and jerked his shaft. I couldn't handle fucking two men at the same time. Not with all the changes to my body. I had so many aches and pains I couldn't even think about anal. So we came up with other ways for all of us to be together.

My body trembled as my eyes darted between my men. I loved the feel of Luca's big dick inside me and Marcello's hands and warm tongue on my skin.

Damian sucked Bastian's cock into his mouth, ripping a few grunts from his throat. His eyes slammed shut, and he looked right at me when they opened again. I smiled, so turned on by him gaining pleasure from my husband. He winked, and then his fingers wove through Damian's black hair, tugging on it hard.

"Baby, look at me." Luca slid his hand beneath my chin and turned my head back to him. "You're so close. I can feel it."

I bobbed my head.

A shudder ripped through me, sending chills down my arms and legs. I rode Luca harder, screaming his name like a sweet melody. And with Marcello playing with my nipples and rubbing my clit, my orgasm washed over me in hot waves of passion.

Lips parted, Luca stared into my eyes as he came inside me. His eyes lowered between us to all the cum sliding out of me. "Look at the mess you made for me."

"Your brothers had something to do with it, too." I brushed my lips against his. "The four of you make me so hot."

He pushed up into me, still semi-hard, a grin in place. "I can feel that."

"You're mine, princess." Marcello dipped his head down and kissed my neck. His tongue glided across my skin, driving me wild. "Let me feel how wet you are for us."

Luca tapped my ass lightly. "Go command your knights, my queen."

I got on top of Marcello, who grabbed my ass in his big hands and squeezed as I slid down his length.

Beside us, Bastian climbed on top of Damian, and my heart raced with excitement. I couldn't get enough of them. So I rubbed my clit and moaned when Bastian licked Damian's length.

I raised my index finger and beckoned them. "Get over

here, husbands." I licked my lips and moaned as Marcello split me open with his big dick. "I need to feel all of you."

Damian rolled onto his side and grabbed a bottle of lube from the nightstand. The bed shifted, and he got behind me, straddling Marcello's thighs. "You're doing such a good job riding my brother." He patted my ass right where Marcello had just smacked me. His teeth grazed my neck as he moved his hand to my clit. "Cum is dripping down your thighs. Who did this to you, Pet?"

"All of you," I moaned.

"I think it was Bash and me," he grunted in my ear, his fingers brushing Marcello's shaft as he slid in and out of me. "You get so fucking hot when you see us together, don't you?"

"Yes," I whimpered when he pushed his finger inside me, rubbing against Marcello's shaft. "Oh, fuck, Damian."

My eyes slammed shut as he bit my earlobe.

"Such a good girl for us, aren't you?"

Pressing my palms to Marcello's chest, I fucked him harder. "Yes, yes, yes."

Bastian fucked Damian behind me.

Before I started feeling the effects of the pregnancy, the four of us had a routine. Luca had rules, so he got to be selfish and fuck me by myself. But Marcello was okay with almost anything.

Damian pushed his finger into me beside Marcello and rubbed my cum on his cock. "That's better," he whispered. "I wish I was inside you, Pet."

"Soon," I promised. "I miss it, too."

He rubbed his cock between my cheeks and against Marcello's dick as he slid in and out of me.

"Fuck, princess," Marcello grunted.

Bastian grunted behind me, fucking Damian like a savage. I wished I could see his face, see how much he loved it. We had installed mirrors in our bedrooms at home so I could watch them. And so they could all see how much pleasure I gained from my gorgeous husbands.

Damian glided his hand over my ass, and heat shot down my arms when he breathed on my neck. My eyes dropped to Marcello, who looked up at me with desire, his chest rising and falling with each breath.

I was so close that my entire body was on fire. A moan slipped past my lips, and it wasn't long before every inch of my skin scorched from another orgasm sweeping over me, shaking me to the core.

Damian wrapped my hair around his fist and tilted my head back, kissing my lips as I rode out my high. "Cum for us, Pet."

Marcello came inside me as Bastian grunted our names. I could tell without seeing him that he was so close. Right about to lose all control.

Damian jerked his shaft harder until his cum coated my ass, sliding into the crack. He dipped his finger in his cum, and then pushed it inside me.

"You're dripping, Pet." His mouth closed over my earlobe, and he sucked. "So full of our cum."

"If only there were a way to have all four of you at once."

"Bad girl." Damian tapped my ass with his palm and smeared his cum on my skin. "Our little cock slut."

"She's our good girl." Marcello kissed my lips, a peck that left me breathless. "Isn't that right, princess?"

I nodded. "But I'm bad for all of you." I glanced at Luca, who sat in the armchair in the corner of the room, naked and smirking at me. "I like when my husbands are savages in the bedroom."

Marcello made slow circles with his hand over my belly, snapping my attention back to him. "I'm putting my baby inside you next."

"I'm all yours, Marcello." I covered his hand with mine.

"After the twins are here, it's Operation Knock Alex Up all over again. Your brothers will have to pull out."

They screwed Marcello out of the deal they'd made years ago. He was supposed to get the first baby, so I didn't get any complaints.

Chapter Five

DAMIAN

H*ome sweet home.*
        The second I walked through the door, I went to find Sofia. I couldn't stop thinking about my baby girl all week, desperate to see her.

"We're in here," Aiden called out from the sitting room.

I grabbed Alex's hand and steered her inside with my brothers trailing behind us. Tears slid down Alex's cheeks as she rushed toward her twin and took Sofia from him.

"Was she good for you?"

He nodded. "The perfect little angel."

Aiden was Sofia's godfather and had been good to our girl. Whenever we needed a babysitter or a night alone, he was always willing to help. Of course, we had Adriana, her nanny. But she couldn't work around the clock.

Alex kissed our daughter on the forehead and then each of her cheeks. "Mommy missed you," she whispered, hugging her against her tits that were so big they were falling out of the top of her dress.

I loved when Alex's body changed. If it were up to us, she'd be pregnant with our babies until she couldn't have more.

We wanted a big family.

Sofia giggled when Alex kissed her again. And then she looked up at me, her cute face illuminated with a smile.

I cupped her cheek and rubbed my thumb across her soft skin. "Hello, princess." Her lips parted, and her mother's blue eyes widened as I spoke. "Did you miss Daddy?"

Another laugh.

"Daddy's girl." Alex put Sofia in my arms, keeping her hand on her back. "She lights up every time you walk into the room."

When Alex looked up at me, palpable energy crackled between us. I felt the shift after we found out I was Sofia's father. I never thought I'd get any of her firsts—because I only wanted to be included.

Over the past two years, Alex and I formed a different bond than what we shared with the others. Having Sofia changed both of our lives for the better. Marcello had called dibs on the first child, but none of us followed the rules. I was glad I didn't listen because if I had, this beautiful girl wouldn't be staring up at me like I hung the moon.

I kissed Sofia's black hair, which smelled like baby shampoo. It was a scent I now associated with happiness. Whenever I caught a whiff, it instantly put me in a better mood.

I still had to work on my urges.

They would always be there.

Some things don't just go away.

I had a family and a little girl who counted on me. So I couldn't be that person anymore.

For her.

Luca tapped me on the shoulder and whispered, "Keep them occupied for an hour. We'll be in the temple with the Knights."

I nodded.

"She can't know," Luca warned.

"I'm well aware."

I hated when he spoke to me like an idiot. Luca treated me like I was a child or another one of his responsibilities. He thought he was the most intelligent person in every room and knew better.

Most of the time, he did.

"I took her blood pressure on the plane," he muttered, his blue eyes narrowed. "It's high. But I lied and said it was fine."

"I'll take care of her. Give me a few minutes to get her outside."

Alex was too busy talking to her brother to overhear us. She was happy for now, and I didn't want to upset her.

The less she knew, the better.

Alex was our queen, and we never lied to her. But we had two little boys to think about as well. Our kids and our wife were our number one priority. So if we had to omit the truth to keep them safe, we would do it.

We all knew Marcello was walking into a bad situation. The Lucaya Group was like a Hydra. For every head you cut off, two grew back in its place. They had cells worldwide and a lot more power than the secret societies. Even the CIA didn't have enough intel about the group.

The only information we'd gotten came from Viktor Romanov, the man we once thought was our enemy. The ex-KGB agent was now an ally and the father of Bastian's cousin, Grace. He gave us everything we needed to take down Fitzy before his death and filled in the gaps about our parents' accident. And then, he led us to Pierre Moreau, the leader of The Lucaya Group.

But he was invincible.

Untouchable.

We only had a name, not a location. Moreau was originally from Paris, but no one knew where he lived. High-profile men tended to stay off the grid, moving between safe houses and living under aliases.

I pushed Alex's curls off her shoulder. "Let's go swimming with Sofia."

She batted her long black eyelashes at me. "Yeah, that sounds good."

At the beginning of the summer, I bought a baby float for Sofia. A natural in the water, she liked to sit under the sun canopy and kick her little feet.

"I have to go back to Wellington Manor." Aiden hugged Alex with his eyes on me. "Pops is expecting me home for dinner."

Alex hugged her brother. "Come see us this week. We need to catch up and paint. I need inspiration for my next show. I'm five paintings short and have pregnancy brain."

"Yeah, I'd love that." Aiden smiled. "How about Thursday? It's the only day Pops doesn't have me doing shit for him."

Now that Carl Wellington was the Grand Master of The Founders Society, he was the boss. He admitted the Salvatores into the society as his first order of business as our new leader. Bastian and I didn't need a marriage or a child to secure our places. Our families' legacies had already done that for us.

After Aiden left, Luca tipped his head at the door, gesturing for us to leave.

I bounced Sofia in my arms. "Wanna go in the pool with Daddy?"

Her face lit up at my question. I could have said anything, and she would have given me that adorable baby face.

"I'll take that as a yes."

My brothers kissed Sofia and Alex before we left the room.

On our way toward the back of the house, Alex said, "I'm not stupid." She brushed her curls over her shoulder. "I know you're trying to distract me."

I shifted Sofia in my arms, so her head rested on my chest. "Can't a man spend time with his wife and daughter without being accused of having ulterior motives?"

"Your brothers are keeping secrets from me." She hooked her arm through mine. "And so are you. You know I don't like when you lie to me. I thought we had a deal."

"I'm not lying to you, Pet."

She rubbed her pink glossed lips together. "No? Because I can tell when you're lying. The muscle in your face twitches. I know all of your brothers' tells. Even Luca's."

"Do you want the truth?"

Alex bobbed her head and blonde curls dropped onto her forehead. "You promised me, Damian. No sugar coating or lies."

I couldn't take any chances with her health. Not with the twins already putting enough stress on her body. Alex still had minor PTSD flashbacks that gave her panic attacks.

My nightmares slowed after Sofia's birth. But I still had them, and so did Alex. Even Bash had dreams on occasion, dark thoughts about the night we killed Fitzy. That was the night he finally let go with me, when he stopped holding back because of his fears.

"I love you." I squeezed Alex's hand. "That's why I made that promise. But you need to trust me when I say we're not hiding anything from you."

I hated lying. But it was a necessary evil to protect our queen and the babies growing inside her.

"Tell me one thing. Will Marcello be okay?"

I nodded, even though I couldn't guarantee Marcello would come back alive. Not when he was dealing with forces outside of his control. His team and the Knights were going into this blind.

That was the truth.

And it hurt.

27

Chapter Six

MARCELLO

We met the local Knights at the temple beneath Devil's Creek. Sonny and his brothers, Finn and Callum, were here. They had offered to go after Drake with us. But we needed them to stay behind and deal with the Irish.

Aiden wasn't an option.

Alex needed him.

So that left Cole and me.

Cole stood beside me with his hands shoved into his pockets, a concerned expression on his face. I understood his pain because I didn't want to leave Alex or our children. The doctor scheduled her C-section for the end of the month, and with all the stress, I was afraid she would deliver sooner.

What if I don't come back?

Luca sat on the throne at the front of the dimly lit room, leaning forward with his elbows resting on his thighs. He blew out a deep breath as he studied each of our faces. "We're in a precarious situation without Drake. He's usually our eyes and ears." His gaze shifted to me. "So that leaves you, Marcello."

"I know Drake's systems."

For years, I'd been learning from Drake. He taught me the basics of hacking and navigating his software. I used his tech

28

for missions with Alpha Command. But none of those jobs ever had this high of a fail factor.

"I can assist," Cole added. "Drake gave me full access to Lovelace. I have the authorization codes."

Luca nodded. "How confident are you that you'll find Drake?"

"We've narrowed his location to a one-mile radius of three possible places."

My brother scrubbed a hand across his jaw and sighed. "We don't have enough resources to send men to three locations."

"Yeah, I know." I released a frustrated breath of air. "Give me a few hours. I should have a better idea where to start."

"Lovelace optimizes over time," Cole told him.

"Tate Maxwell is with Drake." Luca leaned back in the chair, his jaw set hard. "The Lucaya Group will use Tate to get the software from Drake."

Tate Maxwell was an associate of The Devil's Knights. He was also Drake's best friend and head of security.

Drake found Tate and his sister, Olivia, back in high school. They had escaped one of many foster homes and were living on the streets. Even though Tate initially resisted his help, he eventually let Drake feed and clothe them and pay for their education.

"That's not possible," Cole informed us. "Even if they had the access codes, Lovelace is split into pieces. Some of the AI/DL data is on the cloud, where they could access it with the correct codes. But most of the software is on data servers not connected to Wi-Fi. Even I don't know all of the secure locations."

"Tate knows," Luca pointed out. "He's Drake's head of security and would need that information to guard the server sites properly."

Cole nodded to confirm.

Sonny slid his arm across my neck and pulled me closer.

"If you die on me, I'll find a way to have you reincarnated, so I can kill you myself." Sonny laughed. "Alex needs you. We all need you. So you better come back to us in one piece."

"Don't worry about me. I can handle this mission."

Sonny shoved his hand through my hair to mess it up. "I want to go with you."

"No, you're needed here."

"You have a job to do, Cormac." Luca threw out his hand to dismiss him. "Deal with the Irish." He tipped his head at Sonny's younger brothers. "All of you. Go!"

Sonny shook his head, his lips parting as if he were about to talk back to Luca.

I grabbed his shoulder to silence him. "Not now," I said in a hushed tone, begging him with my eyes not to challenge my brother, who was not in the mood for Sonny's sarcasm. "I'll see you when I get back, okay?"

"Damn right you will." My best friend hugged me, patting my back. "See ya soon, Cello."

"I'll be back before you know it."

Sonny gave me one of his pretty boy smirks and left the temple with his brothers.

"The two of you should go back to the house," I said to Luca as my gaze swept over to Bastian. "Alex will get worried if you're gone for too long. Cole and I need to review the footage from Battle Industries and run a few tests to optimize Lovelace."

Luca rose from the throne and straightened his lapels, his intense blue eyes on me. "We'll see you at home. Be ready to leave tonight."

I tapped Cole on the shoulder, and he followed me out of the room. We walked down the narrow hallway lit by wall sconces.

I thought about the first time we brought Alex down here, and she passed out from a panic attack. That was Luca's doing. He wanted to scare her, make her understand she

30

would one day become the queen of our corrupt organization.

"Are you sure about this?" Cole said as we navigated the passage. "Because I'm not. We need Drake to plan properly."

"If we can narrow down Drake's exact location, it's because they want us to find them."

"An ambush," Cole said in a hushed tone. "I figured as much. Look, Marcello, I just had a baby. Hale isn't even a day old. Grace is a strong woman, so she's pretending like this isn't killing her. But she needs me. So does my son."

"I have just as much to lose. We can't fail, so we won't."

I couldn't guarantee anything.

My future wasn't certain.

"Bastian will take care of Grace and Hale if anything happens to you."

As we turned right, headed toward the ground-level access to what Alex called my spy shed, his head snapped to me. "I know he will. But… Fuck, I don't even want to think about the what ifs." His hand cupped my shoulder. "We got this."

At the end of the corridor, I climbed the metal rungs, with Cole on the ladder behind me. I reached into my back pocket and grabbed the keys, turning the lock on the lid. Then I spun the wheel and pushed hard on the metal grate. The security door hit the cement floor.

I pulled myself up and into the room, leaning forward to extend my hand to Cole. He trained at York Military Academy and didn't need my help. So he ignored my hand and climbed out of the tunnel.

We sat at a desk with a dozen monitors. I had feeds of every room in the house, including the backyard.

Alex was in the pool with Damian and Sofia. She pushed Sofia's baby float across the pool with Damian at her side. It was nice seeing him acting like a normal person.

Like a father.

And husband.

I never thought he could change. But Damian was good to Alex and our daughter and would take care of them if I didn't return. So would Luca and Bastian.

At least she had them.

I sat in front of the keyboard, typing the codes Cole provided, flipping between screens at Battle Industries.

"Wait, that's Drake's office."

I narrowed my eyes at him. "I thought his office was on the fiftieth floor."

Cole shook his head. "That's the office he uses for business meetings. His real office is on the fifty-first floor." He pointed at the screen. "This is it."

As I scanned the empty room, I noticed the wall of glass windows that looked like mirrors, shimmering when the light hit them just right. "What kind of glass is this?"

"Drake makes it at Battle Industries. One of his new inventions. It's like the heat-strengthened glass they use on skyscrapers to withstand the pressure of strong winds but with a few modifications that make it impenetrable."

"They attacked this floor. Someone knew about the tech on this level and how to get around it. Is the glass being manu-factured and sold to customers?"

He shook his head. "No, not yet. It's still in production."

"Who has access to this floor?"

"Tate, Drake, and me." He ran a hand across his tired face and yawned. "And Liv has access."

Olivia Maxwell was the younger sister of Tate and Drake's assistant at Battle Industries. They had been friends since high school and were like family to Drake. Although, his feelings for Olivia were not familial.

"Does Drake have other support staff on this floor?"

"No, just Liv."

"Does she have access to his labs?"

"Yeah, of course. Sometimes, Liv has to go in there and

wake him up when she gets in for the day. You know Drake. He's a workaholic and never leaves the office."

"Where is Liv right now?"

Cole leaned forward, the chair creaking beneath his weight. "At Drake's house. She's working at home while Drake is traveling."

I pointed at the logs for the cell phones and computers of everyone who had access to Drake and his software. "Look at the time stamp on Olivia's phone. There's a five-minute gap with no activity."

"Fuck," Cole grunted. "You think someone hacked Liv's phone?"

"She's the weak link, and they knew it." I shot up from the chair and headed toward the steel door. "We need to see Liv. There's probably malware on her phone."

"Drake has measures to block outside attacks." He considered his words for a moment and then said, "But if they were able to kidnap Drake and Tate, I guess anything is possible."

"Where were you at the time of the kidnapping?"

"In my office at Battle Industries on the phone with Grace."

"Cell phone or work phone?"

Cole followed me outside the room. "My cell phone."

"Do you have your work phone with you?"

He handed me his cell phone. I searched for any unusual apps running in the background. Nothing suspicious.

I gave the phone back to Cole. "It's clean."

"So you think Liv is the leak?"

"I do."

"She wouldn't have done it on purpose," he said in her defense.

"I know." Instead of heading toward the house, I cut through the backyard where Alex couldn't see us. "But this is the only lead we have."

Chapter Seven

MARCELLO

I floored the Maserati down Founders Way and headed toward the Battle Fortress. When Alex was pregnant with Sofia, our daughter kicked her every time I took a hard turn. She would punch my arm for every kick, and we would laugh about it.

No matter how hard I tried, I couldn't shake the feeling in the pit of my stomach. This mission was too risky. She was about to deliver the twins.

We built a life together, and I didn't want to lose it. The same thought kept racing through my brain as I parked in front of the call box at Drake's house.

The wrought iron gate rose above the redbud trees. Rosy pink flowers littered the long driveway. From beyond the gate, I couldn't see more than trees.

I hit the button on the box.

"Hello," a woman said with panic in her voice.

Olivia Maxwell.

"It's Marcello Salvatore. Can you let me in?"

We'd previously met, but Luca usually spoke for our family. I preferred to blend into the background and go unnoticed. So I doubted she remembered meeting me. My brothers left more of an impression on people.

She hesitated for a moment, breathing into the speaker.

"Liv, it's Cole." He shifted his weight in the seat and leaned over me. "We need to come inside."

"Oh, hey." Another pause. "I'll meet you out front."

"No, stay inside until we get there. It might not be safe for you."

When the box buzzed, the gate moved inward. All Founders had access codes to each other's gates for emergencies. But I figured Drake's security team would be on higher alert and didn't want to get shot.

I flew up the long driveway and pulled up in front of the glass mansion overlooking the bay. The Battle Fortress always seemed out of place on this block. Like it belonged on the edge of a cliff in California, not Connecticut.

Two men in suits opened the tall glass doors for us to enter the foyer, where Olivia Maxwell paced back and forth. Head down, she bit her nails, stopping when she heard our shoes on the floor.

"Liv." Cole swept her into his arms. "Are you okay?"

"No." Olivia dabbed at the tears sliding down her cheeks. "I'm not okay. They took Tate and Drake." She sniffed, struggling to catch her breath. "I can't lose them, Cole. You have to find them."

"We will," I said, even though I wasn't confident we would find them alive. "That's why we're here."

Olivia stepped out from Cole's embrace and inched toward me. She inspected my face as if searching for something. "You look so much like your brother."

Most people said that about Luca and me. We didn't look like twins, but you could see the similarities. When we were kids, people mixed up our names. They often thought I was Luca until they realized the vast differences in our personalities.

"Do you know where to find Drake and my brother?" Olivia asked me.

"We have a few leads." I held out my palm. "But I need to see your work phone. It might help us narrow down their location."

She gave me a perplexed look, placing the phone in my palm. "How will my phone help you?"

"Because you're one of three people with a top-secret clearance level." I flipped through the screens and found a few suspicious apps on her phone, a clear sign someone had installed malware. "The people who took Drake and your brother are professionals. And they know all of Drake's weaknesses."

"Tate," she whispered, her hand partially covering her mouth. "That's why they kidnapped him? To use my brother against Drake."

I bobbed my head to confirm.

"Oh, my God." Olivia whimpered, her body trembling. "He's all I have left. You have to promise you'll bring them home."

I couldn't make that promise.

Cole snaked his arm around her to keep her from shaking. "We'll do our best. That's all we can tell you for now."

I finished going through the apps and stuffed the phone into my back pocket. Olivia didn't need to know the leak came from her phone. The Lucaya Group knew she would be the most vulnerable. She wasn't experienced with technology or security, making her the perfect target.

"You're staying at my estate until we get back from New Mexico," I told Olivia. "Pack a bag."

She stared at me as if I'd spoken a foreign language. "But... Why can't I stay here?"

"If The Lucaya Group could get to Drake, they can find you."

"I'm a nobody," she tossed back with a slight attitude. "No one cares about me."

"You're important to Drake. And if they can't get what they want from your brother, they won't hesitate to get it out of you."

She scoffed, her hand flying out in anger. "I don't know anything about Drake's tech or his business. I'm his assistant."

"Doesn't matter," I shot back. "We're not dealing with the average criminal. These people are smart and strategic and learn everything about their targets." I looked into her eyes as I said the last part. "You are a weakness for Drake, which means you need our protection. The Knights will keep you safe."

"Knights?" Her eyebrows knitted in confusion. "Who are they?"

"Liv, please." Cole put his hand on her back and steered her down the corridor. "Pack enough clothes for a few days." He tipped his head toward the stairs. "Hurry."

For the past six months, Olivia had been living with Drake as a condition of her employment. He offered to pay off her school loans if she worked as his assistant for one year. The position required her to be at his beck and call around the clock. Everything from morning wake-up calls to ensuring he ate between code sprints.

Drake still had feelings for Olivia. It was so evident in his interactions with her. Years ago, they had a short fling that her brother ended when he found out. Tate didn't want their relationship to get in the way of their friendship. So he made them swear to put aside their feelings.

Olivia touched Cole's shoulder. "Give me a minute."

She rushed past us and stumbled up the stairs, gripping the railing for support.

Cole blew out a deep breath, his eyes aimed at me. "Liv was the leak, wasn't she?"

I nodded. "Found a bunch of malware. She probably

opened a link or downloaded something without realizing it would leave her vulnerable to attacks."

"Fuck." Cole shoved a hand through his white-blond hair and sighed. "Please don't tell her."

"Wasn't planning on it. When we get back to my house, we'll connect the phone to Lovelace and let her optimize the location based on the tracking data."

I heard Lovelace's voice over the speakers. Olivia must have been talking to her because it sounded like she was having a full-blown conversation. I couldn't make out the exact words.

Drake often spoke about Lovelace as if she were a person. A few times, I found Drake in his lab, talking to Lovelace as if she were his therapist. She gave pretty damn good advice.

A few minutes later, Olivia reappeared with black mascara streaks under her eyes with an overnight bag slung over her shoulder. I took the bag from her and headed outside without a word.

"I can't do this." Olivia's voice wavered with each word she spoke. "Tate, Drake... They have to..."

"You're okay." Cole helped her into the backseat of my car and sat beside her. "Just breathe, Liv."

I peeled out of the driveway because we didn't have time to kill, not with the clock ticking.

Tick, tock.

Time was almost up.

Chapter Eight

ALEX

After swimming in the pool, Damian put Sofia down for a nap. I was exhausted, jet-lagged from the trip back from Italy and desperate for sleep. Too bad my mind wouldn't stop racing, my thoughts a scattered mess.

I sat in the parlor with Bastian, clinging to his side for comfort. He held out his cell phone with the call on speaker, so I could also talk to his cousin, Grace. She married Cole Marshall last year and just delivered their first child.

Bastian knew about Grace for most of her life. But he hadn't spoken to her until a few months before Fitzy's funeral when she helped us lure her father out of hiding. We once thought her biological father was the leader of The Lucaya Group. The Devil's Knights were keeping her safe at the request of The Founders Society in case they needed to use her for leverage.

But that was all a lie.

Another bill of goods Fitzy sold to the Knights, a secret that bonded Bastian and Grace. Now, all of us were closer than family. Until I met Grace, I hadn't had a single friend.

"He's so handsome," Grace cooed. "Hale looks just like Cole."

"I can't wait to meet him." Bastian smiled. "We'll come over this week, okay?"

"Send me a pic." I leaned over Bash's arm to speak into the phone. "Actually, can you hang up? I want to call you on FaceTime."

"Sure," she muttered.

I hit the button to start a video call. Seconds later, Grace's face lit up on the screen. Grace had dark circles under her blue eyes, making her pale skin look translucent. She was a pretty girl with long, blonde hair and a heart-shaped face.

"Bash, I need you to promise me something."

He shoved his free hand through his caramel brown hair and sighed. "Cole will be fine."

"You don't know that," she said with her eyes closed, holding a sleeping Hale in her arms.

She was right about him looking exactly like his dad. The beautiful little boy was Cole's twin. He had the same shape to his blue eyes, even the same chin.

"Marcello is going with him," Bastian said to assure her, which only reminded me of what I would lose if they failed. "It will all work out, Grace. You have to believe that. Stay positive."

I would have been much worse if it weren't for my husbands' constant positivity. This pregnancy wasn't going as well as the last one. I had night terrors and panic attacks from the stress.

"I'm trying." Grace dabbed at the tear streaming down her cheek. "The timing sucks. I need Cole at home."

"I know, Grace." Bastian's voice was calm and controlled. "You shouldn't be alone. I'll come over and stay with you and Hale."

They weren't living at Fort Marshall anymore. Grace was all alone in a big house she bought with Cole after they married. She didn't grow up like Cole with live-in staff and everything at her disposal. Even after Grace inherited billions of dollars from Fitzy, she refused to spend it. Bastian helped her distribute the money between hundreds of charities.

"No, don't do that." She shook her head. "I'm okay. Stay with Alex. She needs you."

"We'll come over," I offered. "It's not a big deal. You live around the corner. Besides, we want to see you and Hale."

I needed sleep and a shower, but Grace was my only friend.

"No." She raised her hand to her mouth and yawned. "I'm going to nap with Hale until he wakes up."

I heard the front door slam, followed by several sets of footsteps. One of them sounded like heels clicking on the marble floor in the entry hall.

I patted Bash's knee and whispered, "I'll be right back."

He smiled in response.

I shot up from the couch and poked my head out of the room. Marcello strolled toward me with Cole and Olivia Maxwell between them.

I stepped into the hallway and waved to Olivia and Cole. And when they halted in front of me, I hooked my arm around Cole. "Congrats on Hale. He's adorable."

He held me at arm's length, his face illuminated with a grin that touched his blue eyes. "When did you see him?"

I tipped my head at the parlor. "Bash is on the phone with Grace."

Cole clutched Marcello's shoulder. "I'm going to say hi. I'll meet you out back."

Marcello nodded.

Olivia's eyes were red-rimmed from crying, holding mine before dropping to my stomach. "You're getting so big. When are you due?"

"The C-section is planned for the end of the month." I rubbed my hand over my belly and felt a kick against my palm. "The boys are ready to come out. And I can't wait. They won't stop kicking me."

Olivia chuckled. "I bet."

We'd met a bunch of times over the years at Drake's parties. I caught them almost kissing at his last Christmas party. They had unresolved feelings they didn't act upon for some reason. I asked Drake about her once, and he said it's complicated.

I stood on my tippy toes and wrapped my arms around Marcello's neck. "Is everything okay?"

He gave me a quick peck. "Olivia is staying here until we get back."

"Okay." I lowered my arms to my sides. "I can show her to the guest room."

"Thanks, princess." His fingers gripped my side as he kissed my cheek. "I have to do more recon with Cole. I'll see you at dinner."

Marcello grabbed my ass, making me squeal, and then he disappeared down the hallway.

"You two are so cute." Olivia slung an overnight bag over her shoulder and smiled. "Marcello is super sweet and protective. He's always been so good to Drake."

"I love that about him. It's in his nature to take care of people." I latched onto her arm. "C'mon, I'll give you a house tour before dinner."

Marcello and Cole skipped dinner, which only caused me to worry more. Needing a distraction, I shut myself in my home studio and tried to forget about the last twenty-four hours.

Luca gave me the perfect wedding gift. A studio to call my own, the one place in the entire house I felt at peace. Whenever stressed, I picked up a paintbrush and created another masterpiece.

I was five paintings short for my next gallery showing and needed to focus. Midway through the third song on my Spotify playlist, Marcello entered the room, his dress shoes tapping the floor. I could tell each of my husbands apart without seeing them.

I only needed to hear them.

Sitting in the chair beside my easel, I turned to look at him with the brush clasped between my fingers. "Where have you been hiding, Marcello?"

"Going over strategy with Cole and my team." He sat in the chair beside mine and tapped his fingers on his knee. "We leave in five hours for New Mexico."

I dropped the paintbrush onto the tarp and climbed onto his lap. He rested his hand over my giant belly and rubbed soothing circles beneath my shirt.

"I love you, Marcello." My lips brushed his. "Please come back to me." A tear slid down my cheek. "I can't do this without you. I hope you know that."

He kissed my lips, a quick peck that left me craving more. "Don't worry about me, princess. I've lived many lives. Fought plenty of wars. I've been shot and almost died, and I'm still here."

"Almost died," I added for extra measure since he seemed to think he was invincible. "You barely survived the gunshot to your liver. If my grandfather hadn't been close by, who knows if you would have survived? Out there, you won't have access to medical staff. Anything can happen."

Marcello stroked his long fingers down my arms. "My love for you keeps me going every day. It's what got me through the gunshot wound." He cupped my cheek with his hand and smiled. "You're my wife, Alex. I don't want to lose you or what we've built together. I will always come back to you."

"But what if something happens," I choked out. "What if…"

"Baby, please. Can we spend the hours we have left thinking about something good?"

"Okay," I whispered. "Tell me something good."

"The first time I kissed you." He tucked my hair behind my ear and smiled. "That was one of the best days of my life."

"What's the number one?"

"I don't think we've hit number one yet."

"Why not?"

He rubbed his hand over my stomach. "Because I didn't get you pregnant yet."

"Your brothers screwed you out of that deal."

He nodded. "Bastards. They always get their way."

"I would have married you." I hooked my arm around his neck and sucked his bottom lip into my mouth. "You're my first love, Marcello. I may have said it to Bash first because I was drunk on sex, but I loved you first."

"I know." He nuzzled his nose against my neck. "That's why I never made a big deal about Damian getting you pregnant first. We all got one thing we wanted from you."

"The four of you have given me a life I never thought was possible. When I was a girl, trapped in that hell with my parents, I wished Prince Charming was real. For the longest time, I thought you guys were devils. I'm glad all of you proved me wrong."

"You're so sappy when you're pregnant." Marcello chuckled. "It's cute."

"Please, who are you calling sappy? You whisper sweet things in my ear when you think I'm sleeping."

A blush spread across his tanned cheeks. "No, I don't."

"Yes, you do."

My tongue slipped into his mouth, tangling with his. Grabbing the ends of his hair between my fingers, I deepened the kiss, wishing we could stay like this forever.

Freeze a moment in time.

He rose from the chair with me cradled in his arms. "For the next few hours, you're all mine, princess."

As if I weighed nothing, Marcello carried me up to his bedroom on the fourth floor. Each of us still had our own space, but once a week, we slept together. It was one of the vows they made to me.

Even Luca.

I rarely slept in my bedroom. Each night, I took turns with my husbands. Bastian and Damian stole most of my time. And on their nights, I got both of them.

Damian wasn't as plagued by his nightmares as he used to be, so it was easier for us to sleep together. And he couldn't seem to stay away from us, anyway.

When we entered Marcello's bedroom, I took in every detail of the mural on his wall. A smile pulled at my lips every time I looked at his work. Marcello was so talented but afraid to share his gift with the world.

He painted the Greek underworld with a man at the center of the skull and fire landscape. His head lowered to the ground, dark waves falling in front of his eyes. The man had snakes wrapped around his legs, which slithered up his arms. A king cobra sat on his shoulder with its long tongue hanging out.

"I can't wait to see what you paint on our child's wall." I smiled as his blue eyes locked onto mine. "Sofia's room looks like a fairy tale. And the twins are going to grow up feeling like superheroes."

Marcello set me on the bed and moved between my legs. He put his hand on my big belly. "After I put my baby inside you, we can figure out what's right for our child."

"Sounds like a plan."

He pinned my back to the mattress with his hand between my thighs. "We don't have a lot of time together. I'm not wasting a second. So be my good girl and come for me."

Chapter Nine

ALEX

After Marcello made love to me, it was time for him to leave.

The moment I dreaded.

Marcello held me in his arms and kissed my lips. "I'll be home before you realize I'm gone."

"That's not possible. I miss you every time you leave for a mission."

I hated when he walked out that door to risk his life for others. But, he was my superhero, and it was in Marcello's nature to help people.

Years ago, he saved me.

I often wondered if I would have gotten through the most challenging times with my husbands if not for Marcello. When I wanted to leave, he made me stay. I couldn't imagine my life without him in it.

"I'll be fine, princess."

Luca stepped between us and clutched Marcello's shoulder, steering him away from us. He lowered his voice as he spoke, the pair inching toward the SUV.

Damian moved behind me as if on cue and wrapped his arms around me. "Marcello knows what he's doing."

"I know." I leaned my head back on his chest. "But I hate that he has to leave."

"You get upset when one of us goes into town," Bastian pointed out. "It's okay, Cherry. Your hormones are playing tricks on you."

That was probably true.

"I want to tie you up later." Bastian tugged on my curls. "So does Damian."

I licked my lips. "That sounds fun."

Marcello and Luca walked toward us, wearing stern expressions. Luca wore a three-piece designer suit, making him look even more powerful.

He was the leader of our family.

I felt safe knowing he accounted for every variable. But even when Luca assured me this would all work out, I still couldn't allow myself to believe it. I had a gut feeling something terrible was going to happen.

Marcello bent down to kiss me. It was slow and passionate, the kind of kiss that stuck with me. Long after our lips separated, I still felt his lips on mine, entranced by that kiss.

"I'll see you soon, princess. Paint something new for me."

Arlo escorted Adriana outside with Sofia on her hip. She was a huge help after I had Sofia. My postpartum depression was so bad some days that I couldn't even get out of bed.

Marcello held Sofia and kissed her rosy cheeks. Sofia rubbed at her tired eyes, resting her head on his chest.

It was past her bedtime.

All of our schedules were off.

I brushed her hair with my fingers. "Time to sleep, my little princess."

Marcello got into the SUV with Cole and rode off the property. I stood on the front steps with my family, tears streaming down my face. Bastian wiped my right cheek, and Damian dabbed at the other.

"Luca," Arlo said in a firm tone. He tipped his head at the house. "A moment?"

My sexy husband kissed Sofia's head and then my lips. "I'll check on you later, okay?"

I nodded.

After we put Sofia to bed, I went to the bedroom with my partners in crime. I got on my knees between Bastian and Damian, tugged on the waistbands of their boxer briefs, and licked my lips.

"I want to watch you."

Bastian tilted my head to the side and kissed my neck. "Our dirty queen."

Damian bit the other side of my neck and licked the spot where he sunk his teeth. "My Pet is a naughty girl."

"You wanna watch us first?" Bastian fisted my hair, his gray eyes boring into mine. "Huh, Cherry?"

"Yes," I moaned.

It turned me on watching my husbands together. They always found new ways for all of us to have fun. Luca was vanilla compared to Bastian and Damian. He liked to keep me to himself, his pretty perfect queen placed on a pedestal.

Of course, Luca was just as rough as his brothers. But it was different with each of my guys. Most of the time, Marcello wanted to love me. Kiss me. Make me feel special and worship every inch of my body.

But when I wanted to let my freak flag fly, I went to Bash and Damian. I explored my sexuality with them. We had no limits, no boundaries—only safe words and promises of hot sex.

Damian's lips crashed into mine, his tongue sweeping into

my mouth. Then it was Bastian's turn to steal the air from my lungs.

Between the two of them, they consumed every inch of me. My skin pebbled with bumps of arousal. And with each kiss or pull of their teeth, my body ignited as if it were on fire.

Damian stared at me with the usual hunter's look in his eyes. Like he wanted to tear me to pieces. Bastian was possessive but sweet, brushing the pad of his finger across my cheek.

I threw my arms around Damian's neck. He bit my bottom lip and sucked it into his mouth. Then he turned his head and kissed Bastian. Damian never hid how he felt. Not even before Bastian let his guard down and finally stopped judging himself. He was so worried about what people would think of them.

But no one cared.

It was all in his head.

Until the night I found them in the shower, I wondered if there was more than a brotherly bond between them. I loved that they could be themselves with me.

Damian kissed me again, then let his lips brush Bastian's. My heart pounded like a drum as I watched their tongues tangle and their hands roamed over each other's skin.

Their kisses were angry and primal, so damn hot my insides melted. Damian squeezed his hand around Bastian's throat. And Bastian matched his movements, applying just enough pressure as he kissed him back.

Damian pulled down Bastian's boxer briefs, stroking his cock in the perfect rhythm. They knew each other's bodies as well as mine.

He ripped off Bastian's boxers and pinned him to the mattress. Damian turned his head to look at me as he dragged his tongue up Bastian's shaft. A sexy noise escaped Bastian's throat. His eyes snapped shut, and his hand fell to the back of Damian's head, encouraging him to suck him into his mouth.

Bastian looked as if he were ready to come when he beckoned me with his index finger. "Come here, Cherry."

I inched closer to them.

He patted his chest. "Get on top of me." He licked his lips when his eyes drifted lower, right between my legs. "I wanna taste you."

I was too big to sit on either of them, but they always insisted I weighed nothing. And I loved them even more for making me not feel any different. Like I hadn't gained fifty pounds of baby weight.

I climbed onto Bastian, keeping my gaze on Damian. He lifted his head to stare at me, taking more of Bastian into his mouth.

When I leaned forward and put my palms on Bastian's chest, Damian squeezed my breast. My boobs were massive, twice the normal size. Like every other part of my body, they were sore. But I ignored all the aches and pains and focused on my guys.

Bastian licked me from front to back before driving his tongue inside me, eating me like I was his meal. He gripped my ass, his long fingers etching into my skin. Chills spread down my arms and legs, all the way to my toes.

"Bash," I whimpered. "I'm so close."

Damian gripped my wrist and moved my hand to Bastian's shaft as he continued to drive him wild with his mouth. Our eyes met with each stroke. If my belly weren't taking up so much room, I would have bent forward and helped him. But we had a good rhythm, something we had perfected.

Bastian squeezed my ass, making me come so hard I could hardly catch my breath. Panting, I stared into the haunting green eyes of my handsome prince.

"I want to watch you fuck my husband."

Damian swiped his thumb across his bottom lip with a wild look. Then he tipped his head at the nightstand. I knew what he wanted without words and slid off Bastian.

I grabbed the bottle of lube from the drawer and handed it to Damian. He stripped off his black boxer briefs, his hard cock aimed at me. Giving himself a few strokes, he rubbed the gel on his skin before plunging his wet finger into Bastian's ass.

"Fuck, D," Bastian grunted, fingers gripping the sheets. His eyes closed for a moment, breathing harder.

For a long time, Bastian denied Damian. It took him at least six months after the first time they fucked for him to let Damian be on top.

"Sit on Bash's face, Pet. I want to look at you while I fuck your husband."

I rubbed my hand over my belly. There was something about me being pregnant that got Damian even hotter. He loved seeing me with their children inside me.

They all did.

But it seemed like Damian had a strange obsession. Not much of a surprise, though. Damian had many addictions, and I was one of them.

Bastian pulled me onto his chest. After he got me in the perfect position, he spread my cheeks and licked me. And then, the three of us worked in unison. Damian and I took turns stroking Bastian's cock as Damian fucked him.

My sexy devil's eyelids fluttered, digging his teeth into those blood-red lips. When his eyes met mine, he fucked Bastian even harder. I was so wet my cum dripped onto Bastian's chin.

Bastian lifted me and said, "D, switch places."

We'd done this enough times that we knew the drill. So the second Damian pulled out, Bastian had me on my back, thrusting his big dick into me.

"I have to cum inside you," he grunted, his lips brushing mine. "Fuck, Cherry. You feel good." His fingers burrowed into my hips as he fucked me like a savage. "You're dripping for us."

Damian entered him from behind. And I knew the exact

moment because Bastian closed his eyes and groaned, though his pace didn't falter.

"She's always soaked for us." He bit Bastian's earlobe. "Our queen is a bad girl."

"Yeah, she is," Bastian grunted. "Fuck." His eyes closed. "Harder, D."

That wasn't a word I would use lightly with Damian. He didn't just get harder, he also got rougher. Damian wrapped his hand around Bastian's throat and spanked him with the other hand.

Bastian massaged my breast, rolling his thumb over my sore nipple. "Squeeze my cock, Cherry."

My muscles tightened around him.

"Good girl."

A wave of heat rolled down my arms, followed by an intense sensation that made me shiver. The orgasm swept through my body like a hurricane.

After Damian came, Bastian was right behind him, chasing his high. Damian moved into my view and rubbed his hand over Bastian's ass as he watched us.

Bastian came inside me and whispered, "*Ciliegia dolce.*"

Sweet cherry.

He still played my song for me, especially when I was upset or needed a reminder of happier times. Sometimes, I helped him write new songs.

My husbands lay beside me, naked and sweaty.

I gripped both of their hands. "Time for our bath."

"Yes, boss," Bastian deadpanned, rolling onto his side. "Play with Damian until I get back."

He slid off the bed and entered the bathroom, giving me a nice view of his sexy ass. I could see Damian's handprint on his tanned skin and smiled.

I attempted to sit up, and Damian grabbed my arm to assist. "You two are so good at distracting me. I needed that."

"Marcello will come back to us," he said with certainty.

I gave him a weary look. "Then why do I get this sick feeling in my gut that something awful will happen?"

Damian wrapped his muscular arms around me. "Because you've been worrying non-stop for months about nothing. All of this stress is not good for you or the boys." He ran his hand over my belly. "Marcello will be here when they're born. So quit worrying."

"Let's go, Cherry." Bastian moved to the side of the bed and extended his hand, wiggling his fingers. "Damian is right. You have to trust us, okay?"

I trusted them with my life.

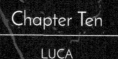

Chapter Ten

LUCA

A lex climbed into my bed, smelling like the fruity bath beads she used each night to soothe her. She'd spent the past few hours with Marcello, then Bastian and Damian.

But tonight, she was mine.

"You look tired, my queen." I brushed the curls behind her right ear and studied her beautiful face. "Ready for bed?"

She bobbed her head. "Your brothers wore me out."

I laughed. "I'm sure they did."

She was exhausted whenever she came back from Bastian or Damian's bedroom. They always shared her when it was their turn with Alex. She rarely spent a night with one of them without getting the other.

Tonight, I was too busy organizing Marcello's rescue mission to lay down the rules with my brothers. So I let them take Alex while I worried about the details. I hadn't heard from Marcello or his team since they arrived at the cave, and I was starting to get antsy.

But I couldn't let Alex know.

She would lose her mind.

I slipped my fingers through her blonde curls and pulled

her lips to mine. "I love you more than anything in this world, Drea."

A smile tugged at her mouth. "I love you, too, Luca."

"I've been thinking a lot about my mother lately. She would have loved to call you her daughter-in-law." Curling my arm around her, I kissed her forehead. "When I was younger, I only cared about my mother. And after she died, I thought I would spend the rest of my life without caring about anyone until I met you."

She grabbed my hand and laid it over her baby bump. "You have changed so much in the past two years. I'm so proud of you. I always knew there was good in you. That's why I never gave up on you, no matter how much I wanted to walk away."

"I promise to spend the rest of my life showing you that you made the right decision."

Alex leaned over to kiss my cheek, the warmth from her breath heating my skin. "You're worried about Marcello, aren't you?"

"Yes," I admitted. "He's the reason you're still here. You wouldn't have given us a chance if it weren't for him."

"And you're afraid I'll leave if anything happens to him?"

"No." I blew out a breath of air, my heart racing as I looked into her eyes. "I'm afraid of losing what the five of us have. You've said plenty of times that it's all or none of us."

I shouldn't have feared Alex leaving us. But at the back of my mind, I wondered if she would still want to be in this relationship if Marcello were not a part of it. This was a concern Bastian and Damian voiced to me earlier. We knew she only stayed because of Marcello. He helped her to see that each of us was worth loving.

"I love each of you in different ways." Alex rubbed her pink lips together, a sincere expression on her beautiful face. "My love for you is not the same as your brothers. One of you will die before the other. That's life. It's inevitable. And it won't change how I feel about you."

"But you said this only works with the five of us," I pointed out. "Many times."

"I only said that because I didn't want to choose. Even if I tried, I couldn't pick one over the other. I would have walked away from all of you. It wouldn't have been fair."

I dipped my head down and kissed her lips. "I think I've loved you from the moment I saw you. Back then, I didn't know how love felt. I just knew I wanted to protect you. To keep people away from you."

She giggled. "You had a funny way of showing how you felt about me."

"I was an asshole." I rolled my shoulders against the stack of pillows. "What do you want from me? I didn't know how to process my feelings for you."

"So you tortured me instead." Alex shook her head, laughing. "And made your brothers harass me daily."

"I know it's my fault," I confessed. "You would have been mine and only mine if I hadn't made the mistake of pushing you away."

Her hand dropped to her stomach as she winced from another kick. "I'm your wife. You still won, Luca."

"Now that I have you, I want to live long enough to deserve you."

Our noses touched, and her lips brushed mine. "How about you show me your appreciation?"

I stripped off Alex's pajama top and sucked her nipple into my mouth. Her hand fell to my head, a soft moan escaping her throat.

"Oh, God, Luca." Her fingers wove through my short, spiky hair. "I love the way you worship me."

I lifted my head, so our eyes met. "Only the best for my queen."

Flicking my tongue over her nipple, I shoved down her

shorts and panties. She whimpered with each tug on the tiny bud that swelled in my mouth. I loved watching her unravel for me.

"Get on top." I flattened on my back, ripped off my boxers, and helped Alex straddle my thighs. "Ride my cock, baby girl."

My fingers burrowed into her hips, digging into her skin. She gave me a few strokes, fisting my shaft as she took all of me.

"Baby," I grunted with each thrust of her hips. "You feel so fucking good."

Alex pressed her palms to my chest to stabilize herself. I took my time, careful not to hurt her. When she wasn't pregnant, I fucked her hard and treated her like my little slut.

She loved it.

But something changed inside me after I found out she was carrying my sons. So I made love to her for most of this pregnancy. And she took advantage of my softer side, losing herself with me.

I propped myself on my elbows and kissed her lips, sucking her bottom lip into my mouth.

Alex was the first and only woman I ever kissed. Until I met her, I never felt the need to show a woman affection. I didn't see the point in intimacy. But now that she was mine, I couldn't stop kissing her.

My skin felt as if it were on fire. And as my orgasm slowly built inside me, a heat wave swept over me. Alex screamed my name when I rolled my thumb over her clit, stealing another orgasm from her.

After her second orgasm, I came hard and fast, my legs shaking from the intensity. I kissed Alex once more, and then she slid off me, laying on her side, staring at me as if the universe revolved around me.

I threaded my fingers through her curls, crushing her mouth with a passionate kiss. "You're the only person who makes my black heart beat." I clutched her wrist and moved her hand over my heart. "I say you're mine, Drea. But I belong to you."

In the past, everything was a game with us. Neither of us would ever relinquish complete control, which forced me to assert my dominance over her.

Alex was right about me winning. Even though I had to share her with my brothers, she was still mine.

My wife.

I grabbed a book from the nightstand, and Alex curled up beside me with her hand on her belly. Our nightly ritual. She bathed and drank camomile tea, and then I read to our sons.

I couldn't wait to be a dad again.

It was different with the twins because they were biologically mine. Of course, I loved Sofia. She was my daughter, too. But she would always have a connection to Damian she would never have with the rest of us.

We agreed to tell the kids which of us fathered them when they were old enough to understand our family was different. Not that it would ever matter, but we figured it would help to explain our unusual situation. Kids at school would never understand why our children had four fathers. Their friends would have questions.

Alex laid her head on a stack of pillows, and I pressed my lips to her stomach. I loved seeing her pregnant with my boys. If she thought I was possessive over her before, it would only get worse when the twins were born.

Alex groaned when they kicked her again. "They like the sound of your voice. I think they're ready to meet their dad."

I laid my hand on Alex's stomach and said hello to my baby boys, feeling them move inside her belly. "I can't wait to see them. I'm dying to know if they'll look like you or me."

"They're Salvatores. Our boys will grow up to be strong and smart and powerful. Just like their fathers."

I cracked open the book and slid down the bed so I could

speak against her stomach. We repeated the same process every night. I would go to my brother's room to find her if she weren't with me. Every night, I read at least a few chapters to my boys. I wanted them to feel connected to me like they were to their mother.

I read *Charlie and the Chocolate Factory* by Roald Dahl, one of my favorite books as a child. My mother had read it to Marcello and me.

We loved it.

I spent most of my childhood in the library, devouring books while Marcello played with G.I. Joe's. We were different in so many ways. And I wondered what similarities my sons would share.

Or would they be as different as Marcello and me? Would they be fraternal or identical twins? How would they look and sound?

Alex brushed her fingers through my hair as I finished the first chapter. Her eyes were half open, but she was still looking at me.

After I read the first three chapters of the book, Alex nodded off. I put the book down, feeling the effects of the past day weighing heavily on me.

Drake was missing.

Our perfect honeymoon was interrupted by another nightmare. It was like we could never catch a break. We couldn't even get married without having a shootout at the ceremony.

Nothing in our life was simple and probably never would be. But now that we were bringing children into this corrupt world, I wanted to shield them. Protect them from all the horrors of our life.

I worried about Marcello.

It had been at least two hours since he arrived at the location. If all went well, I should have heard from him. They should have been on their way home with Drake and Tate by now.

And yet, radio silence.

I set the book on the nightstand and scrolled through my phone, checking messages and emails. Not a single word. So I sent a group message to the team and waited a few minutes.

Nothing.

Alex snored beside me, and I was thankful for that. Ignorance was bliss. I had a horrible feeling Marcello was in danger.

With my phone in hand, I slipped out of bed and waited a minute to ensure Alex wouldn't wake up. She purred with her hand on her stomach, a smile on her beautiful face. Even in sleep, she looked so damn peaceful.

Perfect.

I crept into the hallway and called Bastian. He answered on the first ring, and I told him to get Damian and meet me in my office.

Two minutes later, my brothers entered the room dressed in boxers, their hair disheveled. They looked like they had been fucking around again, which didn't surprise me all that much. Ever since the two came out officially about their relationship, they seemed to go at it like rabbits.

My brothers sat in the oversized leather chairs across from me in front of the fireplace. I drank from the snifter in my hand, eying them up, the scotch burning as it slid down my throat.

I tipped my head and gestured for them to pour a glass.

They would need it.

"I haven't heard from Marcello," I said between sips.

Bastian filled a glass and drank from it. "We knew this was risky."

"Is there any way to communicate with his team?" Damian asked.

"I can't reach them."

"It could be the location." Bastian leaned forward, resting his elbows on his knees. "Maybe they're out of signal range."

"I guess it's possible, but they're using satellite phones."

"They were going into a cave," Damian pointed out.

"Technology isn't always reliable." He sipped from the glass and set it on the table. "Where's Alex?"

I lit a cigar and blew out a cloud of smoke. "Sleeping."

"She doesn't know Marcello is in danger?"

I shook my head. "No, not yet. But she'll ask questions if we don't find him before she wakes up."

"What are we going to do?" Bastian said with concern dripping from his tone. "I'm not about to sit around here and hope for the best and pray they come home."

"They could be dead," Damian whispered.

The three of us sat silently for a moment, not wanting to think about the possibility. For years, I hated Marcello. But after our mother died, I made a promise to her and kept it.

I looked out for him.

I watched over him.

Now, we shared everything—Alex, our children, our business, our home, everything. Losing Marcello wouldn't just kill Alex. It would destroy everything we built together.

It would kill all of us.

Chapter Eleven

MARCELLO

With Cole's help, I tapped into Lovelace's interface and got a rough idea of where The Lucaya Group was keeping Drake and Tate. We knew we were walking into a trap.

But what choice did we have?

Drake was one of my oldest friends and Cole's cousin. Knights took an oath and would never abandon each other. So it didn't matter if this was a fool's mission.

We would find Drake or die trying.

After a plane ride to New Mexico, we followed the coordinates to Drake's location. Unfortunately, the signal was spotty, and we weren't sure this was the right place. But we had to try all available options.

Mark Hauer, my second-in-command at Alpha Command, drove us to the middle of the desert. The small group of us would check the site before deploying the rest of our team. If the coordinates were correct, we were going into a cave. So we needed men on the outside to assess any issues.

As Mark drove across the bumpy terrain, Cole put his hand on my knee. "If anything happens to me, tell Grace I love her."

"Tell Alex the same if anything happens to me."

Cole nodded as the vehicle stopped.

Mark turned to look at me. "Marcello, you're with me. Cole, you're with O'Connor's team."

"Roger that," Cole said to confirm.

Our team climbed out of the SUV, and I joined Mark as we moved to the trunk to put on our gear. We grabbed bulletproof vests, combat helmets, and guns with extra ammunition.

Cole stayed in the rear as we entered the cave. He was about two hundred feet behind me. I walked with Mark and four other guys. The cave was dark, with no light other than our flashlights leading the way.

Mark never showed an ounce of fear. He was a former Navy SEAL, the best on my team. So if I was going into a situation with a sketchy outcome, I was glad I was doing it with him by my side. That brought me some comfort. It also made Alex and my family feel better about this mission.

"I don't like this," Mark said as we crept forward into what felt like a never-ending sea of darkness.

We could hardly see more than a foot in front of us. But it wasn't like we could pull engineering plans for a cave. There was no way to navigate the space other than using the heat maps and technology built into Lovelace. I tried to get the lay of the land before we got here. But even with Drake's tech on our side, I still couldn't predict the correct route.

The men behind us coughed on the dust particles flying through the air. I covered my mouth and cleared my throat. But as we walked deeper into the tunnel, the air became too dense.

"Respirators," I shouted. "Now!"

We put on the respirators, breathing harder as we inched through the cave. When we hit a fork where the cave split into two, each team took a different path. Not long after we parted ways, I heard footsteps behind us and halted.

"Did you hear that?"

Mark shook his head. "I don't hear anything."

Maybe the lack of oxygen was causing me to hallucinate.

We traveled for another five minutes before I heard more footsteps. This time, my team turned around to search the darkness for the source. Even with a flashlight, I couldn't see more than a few feet in front of me.

A bullet sailed past my head and plunged into Mark's forehead, his eyes widening as he hit the ground. I reached for my gun, but the shooter was faster. He took out my team, one by one, leaving me for last.

I aimed the gun at a man well over six feet tall who strolled toward me with an arrogant smirk. He had huge muscles bulging from a fitted shirt that clung to his skin. Dressed in all black, with a mask over his face, I couldn't see more than his dark hair. He had tons of tattoos on his skin, though none I could identify.

A group of men gathered behind him with guns.

"Don't bother fighting us," the man taunted in a thick French accent.

Keeping my hand steady, I pointed at his forehead. But before I could take the shot, something hard hit me on the back of the head.

And then, everything went black.

I woke up with my wrists bound behind my back. Rocking back and forth on the cold, dirt floor, I tried to sit up. But the assholes tied my ankles together.

My head pounded like a jackhammer drilling into the bone. An intense pain that made it hard to keep my eyes open. I looked up at the cave ceiling. The room was dark, save for a sliver of sunlight peeking through a crack in the rock above us.

I had enough light to see Drake's face.

He was a bloody mess, unrecognizable from the man I'd known for most of my life. His dark hair drooped in front of his eyes, ringed with dark circles. Drake wore a suit stained with dirt and blood, the fabric ripped.

"Stop," Drake screamed.

Three men beat the shit out of Tate Maxwell, throwing their weight into his body. He spat blood at them when they took a break. But it only lasted a second before they returned to smashing in his face with their fists. From the looks of it, they had taken turns torturing my friends.

"I'll give you what you want," Drake shouted. "Leave him alone. He doesn't know anything."

All Knights learned how to endure the pain of torture during initiation. Drake knew better than to spill his secrets.

What is he doing?

After one more hit to the jaw, Tate's head lowered to the floor. Our captors spoke in French, which wasn't much of a surprise. The leader of The Lucaya Group was a Frenchman.

When they didn't answer Drake, he spoke to them in French. I wasn't sure what he said because I wasn't like my brothers. I didn't learn several languages while attending some fancy college.

"Give me the location of the server," the man with a mask over his face growled, hovering above Drake. "No more games."

"Don't do it, Drake." Tate's mouth twisted in disgust. "Fuck them."

I wanted to tell my friends it would all be okay. That Alpha Command would be here any minute. However, boulders stacked up the ceiling in front of the only exit, making it impossible to leave.

Without my respirator, it was harder to breathe. I sucked in a few deep breaths and blew them out.

Think, Marcello. Think.

Eventually, they would tire of torturing us, giving me the perfect window of opportunity. All I needed was one hand free to untie myself. Then I could undo the ropes on my ankles and get my friends out of here.

"Fuck you." Tate spat a chunk of blood at the man in front of him. "Do your worst. I'm not telling you shit."

Tate's mucous landed on the man's cheek and slid down to his shirt. His muscular body shook from the anger surging through him like a volcano. He wiped his cheek with the back of his hand and then took the butt of the gun and smacked Tate hard on the side of his head.

Tate had been Drake's best friend since high school. The retired Marine came to work for Drake as his head of security last year. He was built for this lifestyle and could handle himself.

But I was more concerned about how Drake would deal if anything happened to him. Tate would never let terrorists win. He was a man of honor who believed in Drake and his work at Battle Industries.

Several men in dark, long-sleeved shirts and pants surrounded us. They carried enough firepower to blow up the cave and have it collapse on our heads.

"I'll tell you," Drake said after Tate's eyes swelled shut.

Drake was slowly cracking.

As Tate slumped to the side, Drake let out a gasp. His eyes moved between Tate and me. And when he noticed I was awake, a look of relief washed over his face. Although, I was useless to him until I could free my hands.

"Let him go," Drake demanded. "If you kill him, I'm not telling you shit."

The leader of the group waved off his men and moved toward Drake. He held a gun, gritting his teeth. "Give me the program, or I will kill your friend."

Drake glanced at Tate and sighed.

"How do you expect me to do that? I'm stuck in this cave with no access to the Internet."

Tate groaned, using whatever strength he had to lift his head. "Drake, listen to me." His voice sounded like gravel. "Don't let them win. I'll die before I tell them anything." A beat passed before he said, "Promise me."

Drake stared at his friend's bloodied face and shook his head. "No, Tate. I'm not making that promise. You're leaving this cave with me."

"Promise me, Battle," Tate choked out. "No matter what happens."

A minute of Tate trying to convince Drake to honor their deal ensued before our captors went back to torturing him.

"I promise," Drake whispered.

"I love you, brother." Tate's eyes were so swollen he looked unrecognizable. "Tell Liv the same. Take care of her for me."

And when they knocked him out cold, I wasn't sure if Tate was still breathing or if he would ever wake up.

Chapter Twelve

LUCA

For most of our childhood, I hated Marcello. He was so much like our mother. Even-tempered, passionate, not a fucking psychopath like me. Our differences separated us for a long time. But over the past few years, the things that once kept us apart now brought us together.

This family didn't work without him. The three of us owed our relationship with Alex to Marcello. I was the leader of our family, but he was the glue that held us together.

I sat in my office with Bastian and Damian, drinking in silence. None of us could say the words aloud.

What if we lose Marcello?

It was close to three o'clock in the morning when my cell phone rang with a call from Cole Marshall.

I slid my thumb across the screen to answer the call. "Tell me Marcello is with you."

"No," Cole muttered, out of breath. "The cave collapsed. Marcello, Hauer, and a few others are trapped."

I rose from the chair, my eyes wide as I stared at my brothers. "Then send an extraction team. Do whatever you need to get them out."

"We're working on it," Cole said. "But we're running into complications."

"Such as?"

"The Lucaya Group sent men here to ensure we fail." He sighed. "This was a trap."

We knew that.

So did Marcello.

From a distance, I heard gunfire. I grilled Cole for more information, and he explained that the engineers were working on finding Marcello but not without men shooting at them.

"Even if we weren't under fire," Cole said, breathless, his voice wavering, "that's not the worst part. Bullets hit the rock in various places, weakening the cave's structure. If the engineers are off by a millimeter, the cave could collapse on their heads. And even if that doesn't happen, they have a limited air supply. We need time," Cole shouted over the gunfire. "I'll call you back when I can."

The call ended.

I stood there, too stunned to speak. Bastian and Damian rose from their chairs and moved beside me.

Bastian placed his hand on my shoulder and squeezed. "What did he say?"

"Marcello might die in that cave." I stuffed the phone into my pocket and looked at them. "And there's not a damn thing we can do."

It fucking killed me knowing he was trapped in a cave, fighting for his life.

I called my father to tell him the news.

A few minutes later, he entered my office dressed in a black robe and slippers. A plume of smoke gathered around his head as he puffed on a cigar.

"Get Cole on the phone," Dad ordered.

I called Cole from the Spiderphone on the conference table with my dad and brothers surrounding me. The call went to voicemail several times before he finally called me back.

"Is Marcello alive?" Dad asked.

"We don't know for sure," Cole admitted, his voice filled with uncertainty. "If we cut too big of a hole into the cave, it could collapse. The pressure could take the whole thing down on their heads."

Cole was an engineer and had more knowledge than any of us. It was a good thing he'd agreed to accompany Marcello on this mission.

Time was of the essence.

I curled my hand into a fist on the table, attempting to still my nerves. "Can you enter at a different point?"

"Yes," Cole confirmed. "We're drilling now. But I'm not sure how much air they have left. I only made it a few minutes into the cave before I needed the respirator. Marcello, Drake, and Tate have been inside for too long."

"I understand that," I told him. "Let's focus on gaining access to the cave. We'll have a medical team on standby."

"Give us another hour," Cole said, breathing hard. "I'll call when I have news."

I hit the button on the phone to end the call.

My father's deep brown eyes bore into my blue ones. He looked like he was trying to dig through my brain and extract each thought. "Marcello is alive," he said with confidence as he rose from the chair. "He'll come home."

It was almost as if he were saying this for himself. Like he needed to hear the words aloud to believe them.

"Of course." I followed him to the door. "Marcello will find a way out of there."

Dad nodded. He was a man of few words, and at times like these, he often retreated into himself.

He gave me a quick pat on my shoulder and then walked down the hallway toward the stairwell. I spun around and found Damian and Bastian a few feet from me.

None of us had spoken much.

Damian even less than usual.

"It's time to tell Alex the truth," Bastian suggested, running a hand through his caramel brown hair. "She will lose it when she finds out Marcello is lost and might not come home."

Damian brushed his thumb over the black stubble on his jaw. "We should give her a sedative first."

Carl Wellington armed us with plenty of drugs that were safe for Alex to take during her pregnancy. She was so nervous and upset all the time. It seemed like my boys were fucking with her mentally. Alex often joked that it was because they were my demon spawn.

Maybe that was true.

I nodded in agreement. "C'mon, let's rip off the Band-Aid."

After we left my office, the three of us sought out Alex. She was in her studio with Olivia, showing her how to paint. Unlike Alex's work, Olivia's canvas looked like Sofia was attempting to finger-paint. But the girls were laughing and joking about their mess on the tarp.

Alex never had a lot of friends.

That was mostly my fault.

I wouldn't allow anyone in Devil's Creek to speak to her when we were in high school. Even when she studied art at the Rhode Island School of Design, I kept tabs on her. I wasn't that far away at Harvard and had my security team watch her. If she made a friend, I chased them away. Same with men. They disappeared from her life as quickly as they entered it.

Now that I saw the error in my ways, I wanted her to have

friends. A family. I wanted Alex to have everything she never had growing up, everything I denied her because of my hatred.

Alex glanced over her shoulder when she heard our shoes tap the floor. A smile lit up her face. "Why do the three of you look like you're up to no good?"

I smirked, extending my hand to her. "Because most of the time we are."

Damian snickered, shoving a hand through his black hair that needed a cut. A few strands dropped onto his forehead that was so pale it made his lips appear even redder.

"Time for your bath, Pet." Damian hunched down beside her and rubbed the pad of his thumb across her bottom lip. "It's getting late. You need rest."

She let out a soft moan as he touched her. Damian only needed to enter a room, and she was like a dog in heat.

It should have bothered me, maybe even set off my jealousy. But Alex got things from each of us the other couldn't give her. That was the reason our relationship worked so well.

Each of us had strengths. The other made up for our weaknesses. Between the four of us, we were one amazing husband. But separately, we wouldn't have been able to keep her happy.

I often spoke without thinking it through, which led to fights. Damian was impulsive and slightly unhinged. Sometimes, his mental illness spiraled Alex's issues out of control. Bastian couldn't separate fact from feelings and made decisions based on emotion, not logic. Marcello was too nice, too sweet. Alex would have gotten bored with him after a while.

She needed all of us.

And we needed each other.

Alex slipped her fingers between Damian's. He lifted her from the chair, sliding his arm behind her back. Her eyes wandered from Bash to me.

"You can stay and finish your painting," Alex said to Olivia.

Olivia rose from the chair and laughed. "No, that's okay." She pointed at her canvas, which looked like she flung paint at it. "I'm tired. And I have to get up early to handle one of Drake's overseas investments."

She did more for Drake than I had realized. I would never let my assistant handle business affairs on my behalf.

Alex gave Olivia a one-arm hug. "Goodnight. I'll see you in the morning."

After we parted ways with Olivia, we headed to Alex's bathroom. She still shared the space with Damian, even after all these years. It used to give her anxiety knowing he was in the room next door, and now it brought her comfort.

I leaned over the tub and ran my hand under the water to find the perfect temperature while Bastian helped Alex strip off her clothes. He kissed every inch of her bare skin, focusing on her stomach.

She was so beautiful.

Damian raised the teacup to her lips. Alex loved camomile tea because it soothed her nerves.

"Good girl, Pet." Damian rubbed circles on her back with his fingers. "Drink up."

I couldn't take my eyes off Alex and our babies growing inside her. In less than one month, our boys would be here. The wait was killing me.

Alex raised her hand and beckoned me with her finger. "Luca, come here."

I inched closer. "Yes, my queen?"

"What are the three of you up to?" Alex inspected my face for a lie, then turned her gaze on my brothers. "I know when you're keeping things from me."

I took the teacup from Damian's hand and made her take a few more sips until she finished the liquid. "Drea, Marcello is trapped in a cave."

I blurted it out and didn't bother to sugarcoat it. Honesty was the best policy.

A gasp slipped past her lips. "What? No." Tears leaked from her bottom lids and streaked her cheeks. "He promised me…"

Clutching her chest, she bent forward, overwhelmed by the news.

I got on my knees in front of her and wrapped my arms around her. "Baby, we will find Marcello. I promise our kids will grow up with four fathers. Cole and Alpha Command are digging Marcello out as we speak."

Damian clutched Alex's right shoulder and kissed her cheek. "It's going to be okay," he whispered against the shell of her ear. "Give it some time. Marcello will be home by the time you wake up."

Alex glanced up at him, and he swiped at the tears falling. "Do you promise?"

"None of us can make that promise," Bash cut in, standing on her other side, his long fingers trailing down her arm.

"Is he alive? Have any of you talked to him?"

"As far as we know," I interjected, "Marcello is alive."

She hugged herself, trembling from the panic rocking through her. "But you haven't heard from him?"

We shook our heads in unison.

I rose from the floor and offered her my hand. "Marcello will come back to us."

Her eyes locked with mine, once again searching for the truth.

I was right about most things.

She trusted me with her life.

So if I thought Marcello would be okay, she believed me.

She needed to believe it.

Damian's palm circled her ass. "C'mon, Pet. Let's get in the tub."

We peeled off our suits and dropped them into a pile on the floor. The Jacuzzi tub was large enough to seat six people comfortably. At least once a week, we participated in Alex's nightly ritual. For as long as I'd known her, Alex took night baths and drank tea to help her sleep. It was one of her coping mechanisms.

A habit she couldn't break.

I curled my arm around her and pulled her onto the seat beside me. Damian sat on her right while Bastian was across from us. He grabbed her foot and massaged her toes, working his way up to the heel.

I reached between her legs and rolled my thumb over her clit in a circular motion as my lips ghosted her earlobe. "Open up for me, baby girl." She spread her legs wider, and I pushed two fingers inside her. "That's it. Squeeze my fingers."

Bastian massaged her foot, slowly making his way up her leg. He got on his knees at the center of the tub and kissed her leg. Bath time was different in this house. Alex usually got at least two of us, sometimes all of us, and a lot of orgasms. We knew what our queen needed.

Alex's eyelids fluttered from the orgasm building inside her. The tea was already doing its job. Damian must have added a larger dose. Because it usually took her a solid thirty minutes to feel the effects.

She came on my fingers, riding my hand like a greedy girl, screaming our names as her body trembled. I sucked my fingers into my mouth and tasted her. My dick was so fucking hard I wanted to bury myself in her, but she couldn't keep her eyes open.

Our wife laid her head on Damian's shoulder and yawned. "Why am I so tired?"

"Because I put something in your tea," he confessed.

She lifted her head. "You always seem to know what I need, Damian."

This wasn't the first time we slipped something into her

tea to help her relax. She understood our reasons. Besides, she needed the pills. They were the only thing keeping her sane some days.

Alex closed her eyes as Damian hooked his arm around her and pressed a kiss to her forehead.

"Sweet dreams, my love."

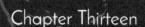

Chapter Thirteen

DAMIAN

I needed a fucking break. Sitting around the house and thinking about Marcello sent me over the edge. Our brother was trapped in a cave, maybe even dead.

Dead.

Dead.

Dead.

I couldn't allow myself to think about Marcello for too long. Not without feeling like my heart was about to punch a hole through my chest. Even Bastian was more distant than usual. He put on a solid front with Alex, but he barely spoke a word when we were alone.

He was scared.

So was Luca.

As expected, Luca retreated to his office and locked the door. He hadn't slept since our first night home. Luca would never admit it aloud, but he needed Marcello.

All of us relied on him.

Without Marcello, our relationship with Alex didn't work. He balanced out the darkest parts of us. Alex would have run from Devil's Creek years ago if not for him. Marcello was the reason we were lucky enough to call her our wife.

So he had to live.

I waited until everyone was asleep and snuck out of the house, flooring the gas to Beacon Bay. The Ferrari hugged the corners as I whipped through the streets, which were desolate at this hour.

My resolve was fading.

In times of stress, I always sought the comfort of my kill room.

It was my special place.

My family said they were proud of me for curbing my dark desires. Everyone thought I had my issues under control. In some respects, I did.

But I still had urges.

On occasion, I had to deal with a body for the Knights. It was inevitable with The Lucaya Group breathing down our necks. I had to dispose of the men they sent after Drake several times. I couldn't deny that I still enjoyed taking a man's life, especially sick and depraved ones.

They deserved to die.

I didn't feel bad.

Luca knew I needed an outlet for my creativity. Sometimes, he would surprise me with a local pedophile or some sick bastard who needed to pay for his sins. They were always evil men who did horrible things to innocent people.

A justified kill.

I parked in front of the abandoned apartment building and flew up the stairs. It had been a few months since I'd gotten the chance to get away from the Salvatore Estate. With Alex out cold from the drugs, she wouldn't know I left the house.

No reason to worry.

She knew I occasionally killed people. I never hid that part of myself from her. But I didn't want Alex to see me like this. Because if she had, she would have known I feared for

Marcello's life. That would start up her panic, inducing even more anxiety.

I opened the front door, locking it behind me, and raced up the stairs. A childlike excitement washed over me as I walked down the second-floor hallway. The same feeling coursed through my veins every time I entered the building.

It was like a drug.

My addiction.

I replaced the high I got from killing with Alex. She had been my obsession since high school. When I tasted her, I couldn't stop thinking about her. Imagining what it would be like to mark every inch of her body. I spent every waking hour dreaming about my pretty little pet.

As I strolled down the hallway toward the last apartment on the right, I heard noises from beneath a door. So I turned the doorknob and stood in the entryway, shocked by what I found on the other side.

A blonde girl with big tits was on top of Aiden Wellington. She screamed like a fucking porn star as she rode him into the couch. Sonny Cormac was naked and on the cushion beside them, biting her neck and tugging her nipple.

The container girl.

Ella Doyle.

Marcello told us about Aiden's history with the girl. That he met her at The River Styx and fucked her one night after the bar closed. Aiden was supposed to talk to Ella—not fuck her again.

I knew Aiden and Sonny were friends. But I had no idea they were this close. None of the Knights had ever seemed interested in sharing a woman. Two years ago, Aiden was against Alex's relationship with the four of us. But now that he was used to it and realized we made her happy, he wasn't so uptight about it anymore.

I knocked on the open door. "Am I interrupting something?"

Ella's head snapped to me, and her lips parted in shock. "What the fuck?"

I wanted to laugh but kept a straight face.

Luca would not be thrilled about this. He ordered Aiden and Sonny to get information out of Ella. Anything we could use against the Irish crime families. We could never have too much leverage over our associates.

"Dude," Aiden groaned, his messy blond curls flopping onto his forehead. "Get the fuck out!"

I shook my head, a smirk tugging at my mouth. Sonny gave me a look that said, *Please don't tell Luca.*

He left me no choice.

We didn't keep secrets in our house.

Shaking my head, I closed the door.

The moaning started up again as I approached the door to my apartment. Even through the wood, I could smell the bleach. We had cleaned and disinfected the space so many times the stench penetrated every inch of the walls, floor, and ceiling.

Fire slid beneath my skin as I entered the apartment. It was my second home—where I could be myself without judgment.

The open-concept floorplan had no furniture. A kitchen to my right where I kept my tools. Pliers, knives, scalpels, the usual cutting instruments. From the look of it, Luca replaced the flooring again. He'd had this space renovated at least a dozen times since high school.

You could still smell the bleach.

That would never go away.

I sat on the windowsill and stared down at the parking lot. A soft glow from the street lamp illuminated the dark street. The Ferrari was the only car in the lot.

Where the fuck did Sonny and Aiden park?

They were too fucking lazy to walk here. Sonny was the epitome of a rich snob and wouldn't walk two feet. And he would never bring his driver here. Aiden refused to abuse any of the luxuries afforded by the Wellington fortune.

They were up to something.

Keeping secrets from the Knights.

Luca would get to the bottom of it.

I entered the kitchen and opened the first drawer, removing my favorite tools. Following my routine, I laid each of them on the counter in a row. Every serial killer had habits they couldn't break.

This was mine.

I liked to organize each weapon, run my fingers across the cool metal, and carefully select my torture method. Depending on the person, I tried to inflict the most amount of pain. The worse their crimes, the worse the punishment. The sick fucks who did shit to women and children received a slow, agonizing death.

Midway through my ritual, my cell phone dinged with a new text message. I already knew it would be one of my brothers.

Luca: Where the fuck did you go?
Luca: Get home right fucking now.
Damian: I'm at the safe house.
Luca: If I have to drive over there, I will kill you myself.
Luca: Cole found Marcello and Drake. They're alive.
Damian: I'm on my way home.

I packed up the tools, shoved them into the drawer, and left Beacon Bay.

Chapter Fourteen

MARCELLO

Strong arms wrapped around me, lifting my lifeless body from the stone floor. My eyelids fluttered and snapped open. White light poked through a hole in the cave the size of a crater, revealing the terrain outside.

Am I dreaming?

Dead?

I blinked a few times.

My arms and legs were useless, so heavy I couldn't stand on my own. A man laid my head on his shoulder and tightened his grip around my middle.

"I got you, brother." He patted my back. "It's going to be okay."

"Cole?" I croaked.

My voice was raw from dehydration.

"Yeah, Marcello. It's me."

After the Frenchman killed Tate, he took turns with Drake and me. They moved on to me whenever Drake couldn't take anymore and blacked out. My jaw felt broken. Every bone and muscle in my body ached. I couldn't see clearly out of my eyes. The lids drooped, making it hard to focus.

With another man's help, Cole lifted me through the hole

in the cave. A member of Alpha Command waited on the other side. He took me from Cole's arms and put me on a stretcher.

Staring up at the sky, I let out a relieved breath.

I made it.

By some miracle, I survived the lack of oxygen, water, and all the torture. An angel must have been sitting on my shoulder. There was no logical reason for why I made it out alive.

"Drake," I whispered as they rolled me across the bumpy terrain toward a medical transport van. "Did he make it?"

"Yes," the man said.

Thank God.

He pushed the stretcher up a ramp and into the mobile medical unit. Two men dressed in scrubs hooked me up to an IV line and pumped something into my veins.

"You're going to be just fine, Marcello," the man said. "We're going to take good care of you."

That was all I remembered before I passed out.

Hours after I escaped the cave, I woke up on a jet. From the look of the interior, it was one of Atlantic Airlines' planes. I sat up on the mattress, surprised to find Drake sitting at the end of the bed.

He propped his elbows on his knees, hiding his face with his hands, sobbing.

"Drake," I muttered, my voice raspy.

His head slowly turned to face me, and his eyes widened. He put his hand on his chest, breathing deeply. "I wish I died in that cave with Tate," he said with pain in his voice. "It should have been me. He didn't deserve that." Drake's body shook from crying so hard. "What am I going to tell his sister? Liv will never forgive me."

I hugged him, and his sobs shook through me. "Don't do this to yourself, Drake. Tate knew what he signed up for when he took the job as your head of security. He died with honor."

"But his death was in vain," he shot back. "He would want it to mean something."

Tate Maxwell was like a brother to him. Growing up as an only child of a tech billionaire, Drake didn't have many friends apart from the children of the founding families.

Once Tate died, Drake lost all will to fight and live. I had to keep reminding him that Olivia needed him and not to give up. She was the only thing that kept him going in the cave.

"Listen to me, Drake." I slid my hand beneath his chin to capture his attention. His eyes and mouth were so swollen he looked unrecognizable. "You did everything you could to save Tate. There's nothing you could have done differently to change the outcome."

"I should have taken his place."

"Those men wouldn't have given you the option," I reminded him.

"I should have given them access to Lovelace." He dabbed at the tears with his shirt. "Then he would still be here."

"No, he wouldn't. The second you gave them access to Lovelace, they would have killed all of us. And then all of our deaths would have been in vain. Tate knew what he was doing. He did the right thing. We won't forget his sacrifice."

"I don't know how to find a global terrorist organization, Marcello. I'm a fucking coder. An engineer. Not a soldier." He shook his head. "We don't even have the resources to take on The Lucaya Group. They will keep coming after us until everyone we love is dead."

"We don't need more money or resources. You have Lovelace."

"I can't do that." He dismissed my comment with a wave

of his hand. "No, it's too dangerous. Lovelace could hurt innocent people."

"You created her. So you can program her to eliminate the threat."

He knew where I was going with this but couldn't accept the facts. If he wanted to beat The Lucaya Group, he had to think like them.

Become a different man.

Losing Tate might have been the one thing to push him over the edge. He had to use Lovelace for evil to avenge his best friend's death.

It was the only way.

Drake squeezed my shoulder. "Right now, I'm more worried about telling Liv that Tate is dead. I can't think about anything else."

The speaker in the room's corner made a crackling sound. "We're making our descent and will land in Hartford in twenty-five minutes," the pilot said.

I tapped his knee with my hand. "We're almost home."

"Yeah." He sighed. "Home."

A lex stood on the helipad between my brothers as the helicopter landed on the blacktop at the Salvatore Estate. My dad stepped out from the group, still dressed in a suit at this hour. He didn't know the meaning of casual wear.

My heart hammered in my chest as the door opened. I sat there for a moment, still in a shit ton of pain. I hadn't seen my face, but it must have looked like it got smashed in with a brick. They hit me for hours until I passed out, repeating the process with Drake.

Dad extended his hand, a worried expression tugging at

his dark features. He never wore his emotions on his sleeve. A trait Luca had inherited from him. This was the closest I'd seen to a physical response from my dad since my mother's death.

I took his hand and climbed down from the chopper.

Alex gasped. "Oh, my God." She turned to look at Luca. "You didn't tell me they hurt him."

I couldn't hear his response.

My father pulled me into a hug and patted my back. "Marcello, my boy." He tightened his grip around me, resting his chin on my shoulder.

That was all he said.

A man of few words, Arlo Salvatore wasn't the type to show emotion. But as he hugged me, I felt his love, grief, and sorrow. He was afraid of losing me.

Drake climbed out of the helicopter, more battered than me. His tanned skin had a yellowish hue, discolored from bruises and cuts. He staggered out of the aircraft, having trouble maintaining his balance. My dad's reflexes were better than mine. He caught Drake by the shoulder and pulled him up.

Olivia ran to Drake. She shook her head in disbelief, staring at his face, and then hugged him.

Drake sobbed on her shoulder. "They killed him," he repeated several times in a row. "I'm so sorry, Liv. It's all my fault."

She screamed so loudly it sent a shiver down my arms. I felt her pain shaking through Drake. They would need each other now more than ever.

With my dad's hand on my shoulder, helping to stabilize my shaking body, I walked toward Alex and my brothers. Alex separated from the pack and hugged me.

I was weak and tired. The medical staff gave us fluids and made sure we were physically okay. But the mental and emotional effects of what they did to us would last forever.

Every horrible thing flashed through my mind like a highlight reel.

Now I understood what it was like for Alex. She relived the worst parts of her life for years.

It took me a few seconds to recognize her touch and adapt to the feel of her warm body pressed against mine. I hooked one arm around Alex, but my movements felt strange and foreign. It was like I hadn't spent years memorizing every inch of her body.

It had nothing to do with Alex.

I was only gone for two days, though it felt like years in that horrible place.

Hell on Earth.

Alex stepped back, running her fingers down my arms, and looked into his eyes. "Marcello, are you okay?"

More staring.

No speaking.

"Marcello." She clutched my wrist and laid my hand on her stomach, so I could feel the boys kick. "Please, say something."

My eyes moved to her belly. Just the feel of Alex and our kids helped to bring me back to reality. Her face and the sound of her voice were the reason I made it home.

I took a deep breath, blowing it out. My eyes widened when the boys kicked her again.

"I'm not okay," I whispered.

She pressed her lips to mine. "I'm here for you, Marcello. Whatever you need."

I kissed her back. "I need you."

Always.

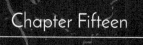

Chapter Fifteen

MARCELLO

I dreamed of blood spilled across the floor, creeping into the stone, stopping right in front of my face. With my head turned to the side, I saw everything.

Each punch.

Tate's last breath.

I still couldn't get the images of those men bashing Tate's head while Drake was on the other side of the room fighting against the restraints. Snot flew from his nose, dripping onto his shirt and mixing with the blood.

Tate Maxwell was a good man.

He didn't deserve to die.

No matter how hard I tried, I couldn't get that moment out of my head. It was like I was frozen in time, stuck in that cave.

With no escape.

I thought I would never see Alex, that I wouldn't witness the birth of the twins or see Sofia again.

But this nightmare was also what disconnected me from them. If anyone understood trauma, it was my brothers and Alex. We had all been through a lot of shit over the years.

Of all of my brothers, I had the least amount of trauma.

Luca shielded me from everything and never let me feel the full brunt of his pain. But now that I had seen the most horrific death I had ever witnessed, I felt different.

I would never be the same person.

For years, I was content with going on missions. I was the leader of Alpha Command and enjoyed that role.

But now that we had children, I wanted to be home more for Alex and the kids. I didn't want to be stuck doing this for the rest of my life.

I woke up screaming for the third night in a row, trapped in that cave. Alex gripped my bicep, calling out to me, even though her voice sounded so far away.

"Marcello." She shook my arm. "Wake up. You're safe. You're home."

This didn't feel real.

It felt like a dream.

When I lay on the cave floor, staring at the puddle of blood surrounding Tate's head, I only thought about Alex.

Her voice.

Her smell.

Her smile.

The way she stared at me when she didn't think I was looking. So many little details about her that I loved.

I blinked a few times to make sure she was real.

She was still there.

"Marcello," she whispered. "It's okay. I'm here. You can talk to me." Alex put her head on my chest, listening to my heartbeat rapidly. "I understand how this feels. It's okay for you to need me for once. You don't always have to be the strong one."

That was what I represented to Alex.

Strength.

Power.

Control.

I never wanted her to feel unsafe or vulnerable. So I tried

to shield her from everything. I loved her so much that I couldn't even think straight when I was around her. And I would have done anything to protect her and our children.

Alex pressed a kiss to my cheek. "I love you, Marcello."

"I love you, too, princess."

She smiled, but it looked forced for my benefit. I could see the tears pricking her eyes. Alex was trying to blink them away. But with her pregnancy hormones, it was harder for her to shield her emotions from me.

She was always so upset.

Lately, it seemed like she was taking on everything in the world and making it personal.

Alex clutched my hand and placed it on her stomach. I couldn't wait to meet the boys, to see if they would look like Alex or Luca. It didn't matter whether they were Luca's or mine because the two of us looked so much alike. Our children would always have some similarities.

The babies kicked my hand.

Alex groaned. "These two are killing me. I can't wait to get them out."

"You're strong, Alex."

"So are you." She ran her fingers down my arm. "It's okay for you to be vulnerable. To tell me anything. If you want to talk about what happened, I'm here for you."

"I don't even know where to begin," I confessed. "What I saw... The things they did. It's never going to leave me."

She nodded. "I still haven't forgotten my childhood. But you'll learn to move on and deal with the pain. It takes time."

"Tate Maxwell didn't have to die," I muttered. "The Lucaya Group won't stop until they get Drake's tech."

"Isn't there a way for Drake to use his technology for evil?"

"Yes, but that's what he's trying to avoid."

"To win a game with monsters, you have to become one.

It's not like Drake has many choices. It's kill or be killed. So Drake's going to have to get over his hang-up."

I bobbed my head in agreement. "For right now, Drake needs to grieve Tate's death. Olivia is mad at him and doesn't understand everything. She doesn't even know Drake is a Knight."

"But Tate did?"

I nodded. "Tate knew everything. He was the closest thing to a brother Drake had."

"So what now?" Alex moved her hand to my heart as she checked to ensure it was still beating.

My heart always beat for her. She kept me going on my worst days. Hell, she kept all of us going. If it weren't for Alex, I didn't know where the four of us would be.

I felt like I was changing.

The time I spent in that cave made me a different person. And I was hoping that she would be okay with who I would become.

"When is Tate's funeral?" Alex asked.

"I don't know. Drake is making the arrangements. Tate and Olivia didn't have any family. Only Drake."

I climbed on top of her and kissed her pretty pink lips, reaching between us to strip off her panties. "I'm home," I said because I needed to hear the words aloud. "You have no idea how much I missed you. I wasn't gone long, but it felt like months in that cave. I love you, Alex. I'm never leaving you again."

Her chest rose and fell as she stared into my eyes. "Do you mean that?"

I nodded. "I'm done with fieldwork. I want to be home with you and our children."

"But what are you going to do?"

"I'll work from my spy shed."

Her eyes widened, lips parted in surprise. "Seriously?"

"Alpha Command needs someone to do surveillance. I can still help them with missions but from a safer location."

I pushed into her, breaking through her inner walls, capturing her moans with my lips.

She hooked her legs around my back and whispered, "Marcello."

I loved how she said my name.

It sounded like a sweet melody as it slipped past her lips.

I slid my hand up her stomach and cupped her breast in my hand, pinching her nipple. Goosebumps spread down her arms, her body so responsive to my touch.

Alex tilted her head back on the pillow. Quickening my pace, I moved my hand between us and rolled my thumb over her clit. Her insides tighten around me, holding my dick in a vise.

"Fuck, princess," I grunted.

My wife bit down on her bottom lip and closed her eyes, trembling as an orgasm possessed her body. She came for me, panting and out of breath.

Bending forward, I left a trail of kisses across her neck. Alex liked my soft and sweet side. But I wanted to take her hard and rough. I wasn't in the mood to be romantic.

I wanted to fuck.

So after she came again, I pulled out and flattened onto my back, moving Alex on top of me. She straddled my thighs, rubbing her hand over her baby bump. It was killing me that I had to wait until my turn to get her pregnant.

Alex rode my cock, and I matched each of her movements. She pressed her palms to my chest, her nails digging into my chest. I circled my thumb over her clit, loving the sight of her unraveling on top of me.

"Oh, my God. Marcello…" Alex cried out, her eyes closing. "I'm so close. Keep doing that."

We worked in harmony together, our orgasms almost perfectly timed. And, after Alex came for me again, I lost all control. The second we both came down from our highs, Alex's lips crashed into mine. A slow burn simmered beneath my skin from her hot, passionate kisses.

I grazed her cheek with my thumb. "I'm not okay, not after what I witnessed in that cave. But I'm going to try to be better for you."

She leaned into my hand and smiled. "Take the time to process your trauma. It's the only way you can let it go."

My wife was the only person who truly understood what I needed. With her, I could be myself. I didn't have to pretend or be brave for her sake. She embraced my flaws and loved me even more for them.

Alex wove her fingers between mine and put our joined hands on her stomach. "I will be here for you every step of the way."

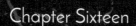

Chapter Sixteen

ALEX

I woke up to Sofia crying, her sweet voice blaring through the speaker. She still wasn't sleeping through the night.

Damian rolled over and grabbed the baby monitor. Sofia was on her back, kicking her legs and screaming.

He squeezed my shoulder. "I'll get her."

"I'm awake," I whispered.

Bastian was on my right side, sliding his legs off the edge of the bed. "No, you two stay here. Get some sleep."

It was my night with Bastian and Damian. We'd passed out a few hours ago after they blew my mind with another one of our wild sexcapades. My sexy husbands sure knew how to spice up our love life. Never a dull moment with either of them.

Since all of us were up, we walked across the hall to Sofia's bedroom. She must have heard the door open because she calmed down as we approached the crib.

Thanks to my husbands, the bedroom looked like something out of a fairy tale. Marcello painted one wall with a scene from Swan Lake, my favorite ballet. I still slept every night to the sound of the orchestra.

The space was a cross between the forest in Swan Lake

and *A Midsummer Night's Dream*. You felt transported to another time inside this room.

"Daddy's here." Damian rocked Sofia. "It's okay, princess."

I stood on his right and pushed the sweaty strands of black hair off her forehead. Her pajamas were damp, so I grabbed a new pair from the dresser.

Damian put Sofia down on the changing table and stripped off her clothes. He checked her diaper, which was dry.

Damian glanced at me. "Do you think she's hungry?"

None of us were baby experts. Even after a year, we were still trying to get the hang of what Sofia needed. I couldn't wait until she could speak in complete sentences or even point at what she wanted.

I rolled my shoulders. "Maybe."

I quickly swapped Sofia's sweaty pajamas for a new pair and sat in the rocking chair with her. Shoving down my top, I moved Sofia's mouth closer. She latched onto my nipple, and I laid my head back on the chair, staring at my husbands.

They couldn't take their eyes off me.

"You guys can go back to bed."

Damian kneeled beside me, his black hair messy from sleep. "I'm not going anywhere."

"Same," Bastian agreed, leaning against the dresser beside the chair.

My guys were so sweet.

Throughout each pregnancy, they took good care of me. They checked my temperature and heart rate, ensured I took my vitamins, and ate on schedule. Luca coordinated every appointment and ordered new clothes when I grew out of them. I never had to worry about a thing.

Sofia ate for twenty-five minutes before she was satisfied. She fell asleep with her head on my breast.

Damian leaned over to brush the pad of his thumb across

her pale, rosy cheek. He loved our daughter more than life itself. Sofia brought out a different side to the man I once feared.

Over the past two years, Damian transformed before my eyes. He still had urges. Those would never entirely go away. But his doctor worked through them with him. Damian credited his new outlook on my love for him. Although, I thought Sofia was the one who saved him.

Damian took her from my arms and laid her in the crib with care. "I'm going to stay with Sofia." He dropped to the full-size bed where we slept some nights. It was easier when she was a newborn and waking us up all night. "Go back to bed."

Damian propped himself up with his elbow, eyes on Sofia's crib. Of all my husbands, he was the most attractive. It always struck me as odd that someone so beautiful on the outside could have so much darkness inside. That side of Damian kept most people away.

But not me.

I saw right through him.

Bastian hovered over Sofia's crib and watched her sleep. His caramel brown hair was longer than usual, forcing him to push it off his forehead. He hadn't gotten a haircut lately or even shaved.

All the stress with Drake and Marcello was wearing on all of us. I saw the signs with each of my husbands.

Bastian barely slept and had dark circles under his eyes. I was partly to blame for that. Most nights, I woke up with heartburn or stomach pains from gas. Sometimes, it was the boys kicking me too hard. There were dozens of reasons why I couldn't sleep.

I was constantly stressed, counting the days until the twins' delivery. Our entire house was restless. Especially now that Marcello was home. He was up a lot with nightmares and horrible memories from what he witnessed in the cave.

He felt personally responsible for what happened to Drake. Even blamed himself for Tate's death. Marcello thought it was his job to protect everyone but never worried about himself. We were all concerned with his mental health and the lasting effect of the trauma.

The Lucaya Group had cast a dark cloud over our heads. We couldn't seem to get out from under it.

After Damian fell asleep beside me, Bastian extended his hand, wiggling his fingers. He helped me up from the bed and wrapped his arm around me. "Time for bed, Cherry."

I took one last look at Damian.

He looked so peaceful with his arm tucked underneath his head, snoring softly. He rarely slept before we had kids, so I didn't want to wake him.

Bastian tugged on my hand and whispered, "Let's go. Damian will come back to bed when he wakes up."

Since Sofia's birth, Damian had been sleeping in her room when he wasn't with Bash and me. He said he wanted to be closer to his daughter.

He loved her more than anything in this world, maybe even more than he loved me. And I was perfectly okay with that. I wanted him to have that kind of relationship with our daughter.

Bastian guided me back to his room, and we got into bed. I rolled onto my side, unable to get comfortable.

He flicked off the bedside lamp and curled onto his side to face me. His breath warmed my cheek as he kissed my skin. "Night, Cherry"

"Can you turn on Swan Lake? I'm going to fall asleep easily."

"I'm wide awake."

The mattress shifted beneath his weight a second later, and a soft light bathed the room. Bastian sat up and pulled me into his warm embrace, making me feel safe.

I loved this about him.

He was aggressive and possessive, a hunter like Damian, but also soft and sweet. A side to him few people got to see.

"Swan Lake," I reminded him.

"How about I do you one better? I've been working on a new song for you."

"You have?" My voice reached a higher octave, surprised by his confession. "What's it called?"

He shrugged. "I won't know until I finish the song."

"Well, let's hear it."

Bastian slid off the bed and led me over to the grand piano. He'd created new songs for me. But nothing spoke to me like the first song he ever wrote for me.

Sweet cherry.

It was personal.

He wrote *Ciliegia dolce* when he was at his worst. Even though Bastian was nicer to me than Luca and Damian, he was still an asshole back then. It wasn't until he wrote that song, and his walls came crumbling down, that I saw there was a lot more to Bastian Salvatore than expected.

"Put your hands on top of mine," Bastian instructed.

I felt the beautiful but haunting notes as his hands moved across the keys. It sounded like a mixture of *The Phantom of the Opera* and *Wicked*. I loved both musicals. Bastian's song had a magical feel. And as he played, I forgot about our troubles, letting them slip away.

"This is beautiful, Bash," I whispered when he finished the song. "Absolutely perfect. As usual, you never disappoint."

He slipped his hand through my hair, and his lips brushed mine. Our noses touched. We breathed against each other's lips for a moment.

"I love you, Cherry." He gave my lips a quick peck. "You have given me some of the happiest moments of my life. I will cherish them forever."

"Why are you talking like you're leaving… or something is wrong?"

His broad shoulders rose a few inches. "Almost losing Marcello put things into perspective for me. It made me realize the same thing could happen to any of us. You need to know I love you."

"You show me with your actions every day. I don't need to hear the words to know the truth."

He raised my hand to his lips and kissed my skin. "I'm so scared of losing you."

"That won't happen." I forced a smile for his benefit. "I'm staying right here with you."

Lately, all of us have been feeling the effects of Marcello's forced captivity. Add in Drake's kidnapping, Tate's death, and the threat of The Lucaya Group.

I would never feel safe.

None of us would.

The Salvatore brothers gave me everything I ever wanted. So if that meant having to face occasional attacks, it was worth it.

After Bastian played a few more songs for me, we went back to bed. He turned on Swan Lake and lit another candle.

For as long as I could remember, this was my nightly ritual. Something I did to help soothe my nerves. I'd adopted many coping mechanisms: music, painting, chamomile tea, and a bath before bed.

Bastian turned onto his side behind me, resting his chin on my shoulder. He placed his hand over my stomach.

"I can't wait until it's my turn," he whispered. "I've been thinking about getting you pregnant since I killed Fitzy."

"Why then?"

"Killing my grandfather allowed me to take back the parts of myself he stole from me."

"I had no idea."

"When he died, a part of me died with him," Bastian confessed. "There was a lot of hatred inside him. He polluted my mind after my parents died. Fitzy convinced me that my feelings didn't matter. The internal voice of my grandfather held me back."

"You've done well, Bash. Don't discount the progress you made on your own."

"I didn't realize how much I wanted a family of my own until after he died." Bastian nibbled on my earlobe. "I want to have a family with you."

"We have a family," I said in a hushed tone. "Sofia is your daughter." I clutched his hand right over where the boys kicked me. "The twins are yours, too."

"You know what I mean, Cherry. I will always treat our children as if they are biologically mine. But I want a kid with you."

"I get it."

But did I?

I hadn't considered the arrangement from my husbands' view. They made it seem so effortless. Like they were always meant to be in a polyamorous relationship with me.

"Marcello is next."

"I know." He sighed. "Then you're all mine."

"I can't wait to have your baby."

"It will be worth the wait." He rubbed my stomach. "I'm just glad to have everyone at home."

"You were worried about Marcello, huh?"

Until now, he hadn't mentioned a single word about what happened to Marcello. Instead, he acted as if he were unaffected.

They all did.

"Yeah," Bastian muttered. "I'm all fucked up over Marcello. He could have died in that cave. We could have lost him forever."

"Do you want to talk about it?"

"None of us are okay, not even Luca. He holds it all in and acts like everything is fine. Losing Marcello would have killed him, too."

"You need each other," I pointed out. "It's okay to need your brothers. The same blood doesn't have to run through your veins for you to be a family."

Bastian's cheek pressed against mine, his tears wetting my skin. "Family is the most important thing to me."

"All of you went through childhood trauma together, horrible things other people won't understand. And it bonded you."

"It did," he agreed.

"You love them, Bash. And they love you."

"I don't know what to do. I don't know how to help Marcello. He's been struggling and won't talk to any of us."

For the past two weeks, Marcello had only talked to me about his experience. He woke up every night sweaty and out of breath. Some nights, he even thought I was the enemy until he snapped out of it.

"Maybe it's your approach," I suggested. "Show this side of yourself. It will help Marcello feel like he can talk to you."

"You know how men are." He laughed. "We don't know how to do this. Feelings and all that shit."

"Yes, you do. You're doing it with me right now."

"Damian thinks we should go to family counseling." Bastian slid his fingers up and down my arm in a soothing motion. "What do you think?"

I could hear the frustration in his tone. He didn't want to admit that he needed help. None of them did.

"There's nothing wrong with needing professional help," I told him. "Damian has learned how to cope with things better because of his doctor."

Bastian nodded. "He doesn't need me as much as he used to. I think you had a lot to do with him changing. So did Sofia."

"We can only help him so much," I said because he needed to hear it. "Damian has done a lot of the work on his own, and it's because his doctor knocks a lot of sense into him.

He's not always perfect. Damian has moments when I see him slip back into old patterns."

"So you think we should all go?"

"I have spent most of my life working through issues with my doctors. They talked me off the ledge when I felt like I was losing my mind."

"Okay," Bastian agreed. "I'll go to the doctor, but only if my brothers go with us."

"That's a good idea." I smiled in the darkness. "We should go as a family."

My eyelids fluttered, overwhelmed by the exhaustion taking over me. Swan Lake was midway through the ballet. The candle flicked, slowly dimming on the nightstand. We must have been talking for a lot longer than I realized.

I rolled onto my side and kissed him. "Goodnight, Bash."

"Sweet dreams, Cherry."

Chapter Seventeen

MARCELLO

I found Alex sitting in front of an easel in her studio. After Luca had surprised her with the space, she wanted to get started on her fresco. But with her going from one pregnancy to the next, the ceiling was still white and bare.

I wanted to help her with it.

Alex leaned forward in a comfortable chair, the paintbrush gliding across the canvas. I loved watching my wife in her element. She reminded me of the best days of my childhood when my mother was still alive.

My mom would have loved her.

When I was a kid, I would sit in my mother's studio chair and watch her paint. She would have her hair pinned up with paintbrushes, her dark hair falling into her face. Paint on her skin and clothes, even in her hair.

She always looked happy in that room, like it was her favorite place. That was how Alex looked when she painted. Not a care in the world, my wife let go and created masterpieces.

I never thought I would marry for love.

My parents did, but in our world, most of us had to marry

JILLIAN FROST

for power. I was lucky and so damn thankful to be home with
Alex.

With my family.

As I walked toward her, I lifted a paintbrush from a table,
rolling it between my fingers. She'd been asking me to paint
with her for years.

I finally felt ready.

It was time.

"Which of my husbands is spying on me?" Alex chuckled,
her back to me, the brush sweeping across the canvas.

"I want to paint with you."

She startled at my confession, turning to the side with her
lips parted in shock. "Are you serious?"

I nodded. "I could use the stress release."

Alex had gotten into painting as an outlet for her trauma.
It was a suggestion from her therapist. And since I still wasn't
feeling like myself, Alex talked all of us into seeing a doctor.

We spoke about Alex and my mother, about how much I
loved painting but wasn't allowed to pursue it because of my
father.

Dad was just happy to have me back. He didn't even
protest when I resigned as the leader of Alpha Command and
trained my replacement without asking him. Even Luca was
on board with my new role within the family. So if I wanted to
paint, they wouldn't stop me.

I no longer cared what anyone thought.

Alex rose from the chair. "I've been waiting for this day for
a long time. What changed your mind?"

I gripped her hip and pulled her closer. "I don't have to
pretend to be someone else anymore."

"You never hid from me." Her hands slid up my chest. "I
always saw you for what you are. An artist." She rubbed her
red-glossed lips. "Like calls to like."

"What are you working on?"

She glanced over her shoulder at the canvas. "Something

for my gallery showing. I still have one more painting to go. Wanna help me?"

I bobbed my head. "I am your humble servant."

Alex giggled and tugged on my hand, leading me to the canvas. She told me which colors she needed, and I refilled the pallet and handed it to her.

Alex twirled the brush between her fingers, eyes on me. "I have a better idea. How about you paint me?"

I raised a curious eyebrow. "What do you have in mind?"

"Paint me how you see me." A smile touched her eyes. "Real art comes from emotion, expression. Let your creativity guide you."

I loved when she looked at me like I was the center of her universe. She believed in me more than anyone else in this world. And I loved her even more because of it. No matter what, Alex never gave up on me.

I still wasn't feeling like myself.

A few nights, I woke up with my hand around her throat, pinning her to the bed. I was lost in a nightmare, convinced she was the enemy. Not until she screamed my name did I snap out of it. The sound of her voice was enough to bring me back to reality.

She didn't get mad.

Quite the opposite.

"Take off your dress."

She started wearing dresses once she hit the third trimester. Alex said other clothes didn't feel right on her body.

I placed a new canvas on the easel and prepared the paint selection. Alex's dress hit the floor by my feet.

Resting her elbow on the arm of the chair, she put her fist under her chin and stared at me. "You like watching me work. But I enjoy moments like this one with you. You look at peace when it's just us in this studio."

I sat in front of the easel, my eyes on her beautiful body. "That's how I feel when I'm with you."

Alex wet her lips with her tongue. "I love that I have something special with each of you. Sometimes, it must be hard for the four of you to share me."

I dipped a rigger brush into black paint. "At first, it was hard. We wanted you all to ourselves. But this relationship only works with the five of us."

"Yeah," she agreed. "It does. And I'm glad because I don't think I would have been able to choose between you."

I traced the outline of her body on the canvas. "Who are you kidding, princess? You would have picked me."

She giggled, readjusting her position on the chair. "So confident."

"We both know it." I smirked. "Just admit it."

Alex's eyes lit up as they met mine. "I plead the fifth."

After that, she sat in silence, allowing me to think about how I wanted to reveal each of her features. She had a perfect heart-shaped face and high cheekbones.

Such a natural beauty.

So I painted her the way she appeared in my mind. Her face was the last I saw when I was in and out of consciousness in that cave. But, thinking about her kept me going.

She was the reason I survived.

We sat silently for close to an hour before Alex needed to pee. I helped her up from the chair and followed her into the room attached to her studio.

Luca added the bathroom after she got pregnant with the twins. I was surprised she made it through an hour-long sitting. Only a bit longer, and I would have finished her painting.

I usually couldn't paint this fast. But Alex inspired me, the perfect muse, so my paintbrush flew across the canvas.

After she finished up in the bathroom, Alex resumed her place in the chair. She leaned forward to peek at the canvas and gasped.

"Marcello." Her hand covered her mouth. "Wow! This is incredible. Your best work yet."

Her approval meant everything to me.

"I take it you like it."

"I love it." She rose from the chair and hugged me, smiling. "It's brilliant. Is this really how you see me?"

I nodded. "You're the queen of my world."

I painted Alex wearing a white toga, one breast showing. A golden crown floated above her head. She held out her hands and summoned fire from the underworld. I stood behind her with my hand on her right shoulder, Luca's hand on the other side. Damian and Bastian were on their knees in front of her, pulling her thighs apart, worshiping their queen.

We were mostly naked, apart from the greaves covering our legs. It was the most provocative thing I'd ever painted. Not something I could hang in any of the downstairs rooms of the house.

It captured Alex and her knights perfectly.

A tear leaked from her bottom eyelid and dripped down her cheek. I brushed her skin with my thumb and heat rushed down my arm like wildfire.

Fisting her curls, I pulled her mouth to mine.

"Marcello," she whispered.

"Say it again."

"Marcello."

I fucking loved it.

Throwing her arms around my neck, she kissed me like she was trying to steal the air from my lungs. With her naked body on display and teasing me, I massaged her nipple.

She squealed.

"Did that hurt?"

"No, I'm sensitive."

I sucked her sore nipple into my mouth.

Alex whimpered. "That feels good."

I guided her to the chair and moved between her spread thighs. She arched her back, lifting her hips.

"I feel like a queen with you." She shoved her fingers through my hair and tugged at the ends. "You always make me feel special, Marcello."

I devoured her like a starving animal, and her eyes slammed shut when I flicked my tongue over her clit. She screamed my name, pulling on my hair. And with each second she got closer to release, she yanked harder.

My tongue went deeper and deeper, tasting every inch of her. She writhed beneath me, whispering my name on repeat. Her legs shook, and her orgasm spilled out of her, coming so hard she struggled to catch her breath.

Alex draped her right leg over my shoulder. "I'd like you to fuck me now."

I laughed. "Oh, would you?"

She licked her lips. "Yes. And then we can finish painting."

Before I entered the studio, I was depressed and struggling with flashbacks from the cave. With my wife, I felt like I could do anything, be anyone.

Alex saw the real me.

Chapter Eighteen

MARCELLO

On the outside, Drake looked the same, but losing Tate changed him. We sat side by side in the Battle Cave hidden beneath the main house. Drake had dozens of computers and monitors spread throughout the room. More gadgets than I could count.

"If you miss this line"—Drake pointed at the screen—"you'll get an error."

"So make sure I don't miss it." I smirked. "Got it, Battle."

"You're a fast learner." He sat back in the gaming chair and turned to face me. "Even Cole hasn't picked up some of this stuff, and he's an engineer."

"I'm proof you don't need college to do cool shit."

He laughed. "I'm hungry. Stay for lunch."

"Sure." I shrugged. "I can eat."

Alex expected me home soon, but I could spare another thirty minutes for one of my oldest friends. Without Tate, he only had Olivia. And even though she still worked for him, they weren't on the best terms. She only spoke when he addressed her directly.

We took the elevator from the secret lab in Drake's basement to the ground floor. This place was like something out of a comic book. Screens and motion sensors were everywhere. Lovelace could hear you anywhere in the house and respond if you spoke. She was more intelligent than any person and could extract information within seconds.

Cameras followed us as we walked down a long marble hallway and into the kitchen. Drake had doubled his security team and still hadn't returned to Battle Industries. Cole was holding down the fort at headquarters while Drake recovered.

He had dark bruises on his face that were starting to turn yellow. His eyes had rings around them, but at least he could open them now. Drake was in bad shape after we got home. I was happy to see him returning to his old self.

When we entered the kitchen, Olivia angled her body to look at us, a scowl plastered on her face.

"Liv," Drake said as he inched toward her, like a kitten taking slow, tentative steps toward a lion. "It's lunchtime. You should eat with us."

She shook her head. "No, I'm not hungry."

He moved beside her and clutched her shoulder. "You keep saying that. But you must be hungry."

Olivia shoved his hand away and stepped out of his reach. "I feel sick to my stomach. And I don't want to eat." With her head down, she sniffed back tears. "Go wait in the dining room. I'll coordinate with the chef."

For the next few months, Olivia was still his assistant. She did everything from wake-up calls to making travel arrangements. Anything Drake needed, she handled.

The situation was no longer healthy for either of them. They used to joke and tease each other. Now, they could barely stand to be in the same room.

We sat in the dining room in silence for several minutes before Drake spoke.

He put his face in his hands and sighed. "I can't do anything fucking right, Marcello. She hates me. I have all the money in the world. I can figure out any problem." He lifted his head and had tears in his eyes. "But I can't bring her brother back. It's fucking killing me."

"You did everything you could to save Tate."

I heard the butler's kitchen door open and heels tapped on the tiled floor.

"You could have told Tate to stay in the Marine Corps." Olivia dropped our plates onto the table with a clang. "You could have refused to let him work for you. He's dead, and it's all your fault, Drake! I wish we never fucking met you. We would have better off on the streets."

Before he could respond, she ran out of the room.

"Fuck." Drake shot up from the chair, wiping his eyes. "Do you see what I'm talking about? She's like family. But I can't even breathe without her yelling."

I pulled him into a hug because he looked like he needed one. Drake wrapped his arms around me and sobbed on my shoulder. We stayed that way until he stopped trembling.

"I'm sorry." Drake stepped back, running his fingers through his dark hair. "I don't want you to see me like this."

"Don't be sorry. I was a mess when I got home. If it weren't for Alex, I would still feel like I'm losing my mind." I patted his shoulder. "You and Liv need each other. It's going to take time for her to see that."

"She's never going to forgive me." He dabbed at his face with the Batman T-shirt hidden beneath his black suit. "Liv is only here because of the deal we made. I want to tell her she can go, but I'm afraid of what will happen." He resumed his place at the table and put a cloth napkin on his lap. "At least while she's living under my roof, I can keep an eye on her."

I lifted the fork and sliced into the meat. "You're making the right call."

Drake nodded. "I hope so."

"You have to avenge her brother's death," I said between bites of steak. "I know you're resistant to using Lovelace to start a war. But it's the only way our families and the Knights will ever be free of The Lucaya Group."

He dropped the fork onto the plate and wiped his mouth with a napkin, throwing it onto the table. "We talked about this, Marcello."

"You'll be doing the world a service." I held his gaze, maintaining a stern expression. "The Lucaya Group has to go."

"I don't see you offering to help," he shot back with anger dripping from his tone. "If this goes wrong, it's my ass on the line."

"I will help you. So will the Knights. But we need you to lead us."

Drake was the only person who could code and optimize Lovelace to eliminate The Lucaya Group. And until now, he didn't have to proper motivation to use the software for evil.

I woke up from another nightmare in the middle of the night, only to find Alex missing. She was soundly sleeping beside me when I passed out.

And now, she was gone.

I got out of bed and checked every floor until I found her in the kitchen. She often ended up down here when she had a craving and didn't want to wake one of us.

The soft light from the open refrigerator illuminated her baby bump as she drank straight from the milk carton. I laughed as I crossed the room.

"Hey, don't judge me."

I took the milk from her hand and pulled my beautiful wife into my arms. "How are you feeling?"

"Hungry." She yawned, rubbing her eyes. "Tired. But

mostly scared. It was hard enough delivering one baby, let alone two."

"It'll be okay, princess." I ran my hand down her back to soothe her. "We're prepared for the boys. You have nothing to fear."

She stood on her tippy toes, and her lips crashed into mine. Slipping her tongue into my mouth, she tugged on the ends of my hair, deepening the kiss.

Our hot moment of passion ended when liquid wet my bare feet.

She peeled her lips from mine, eyes wide. "My water broke. But my C-section isn't for a few more days." She waved her hand in front of her face. "I'm not ready."

"Listen to me." I clutched her shoulders. "You can do this. Same as last time. We'll be there with you the entire time."

"I need a shower," she said with a sour face, standing in a puddle of amniotic fluid.

I texted my brothers and got Alex into the elevator. We rode it to the second floor, where Damian and Bash met us in the bathroom.

"I'm wet," Alex groaned.

Damian pulled the nightgown over her head. "It's okay, Pet. Let us take care of you."

Bastian ran the water and got in the shower with Alex and Damian.

Luca entered the bathroom a second later, dressed in black Dolce & Gabbana boxer briefs. He didn't undress and got into the oversized stall with them. So I figured fuck it and didn't bother either.

My older brother rubbed his hand over her stomach and bent down to wash her legs. "Deep breaths," Luca reminded her. "You're okay, Drea. We got you."

Since the twins were his, we let him take control. He wanted to do everything for Alex. It was his right as the biological father. We all stepped aside for Damian when

Sofia came into his life. The same would apply to Bastian and me.

Alex put her hand on his shoulder. "Is the doctor on her way?"

"Yeah, baby." Luca rose to his full height after cleaning the lower half of her body. "She'll be here soon. Nothing to worry about. You have plenty of time before the twins come."

Bastian and Damian each gripped one of her arms to keep her steady. She was shaking, her nerves getting the best of her.

I moved to Luca's side and brushed my thumb across her cheek. "You're the strongest woman I know. Remember that, princess."

She leaned into my hand and smiled.

"Marcello is right," Luca agreed. "We talked about this. I planned every second of the birth with your doctor. She has this under control."

Alex wanted to have the boys at home, but she also feared something horrible happening. So Luca designed an operating room to the doctor's specifications. My brother had accounted for every variable. Carl Wellington would also be here for the birth just in case we needed a surgeon.

We got out of the shower.

Luca towel dried Alex's body, getting every last drop of water. He was so good with her. I never thought I would see Luca on his knees for anyone, let alone a woman.

He adored our queen.

We all did.

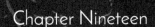

Chapter Nineteen

ALEX

I was a mom again. This time, to two of the cutest baby boys. Michelangelo and Leonardo Salvatore—the heirs to our empire.

Leo had my blonde curly hair, while Angelo's was black like his father. They looked like Luca's baby pictures, down to the curve of his face. The same nose, even the same denim blue eyes. They could also pass as Marcello's sons.

I sat beside Luca on the couch in the twins' room, cradling our tired boys in our arms. Luca held open a collector's edition of *Peter Pan* that his mother had read to him, speaking aloud for everyone to hear.

Bastian and Marcello leaned against the wall beside Damian, who held Sofia against his chest. She'd already dozed off, but the sound of Luca's voice seemed to comfort all of our children. We did this every night for the past two months.

Tonight was special.

We were leaving Devil's Creek to have some fun at The Mansion. It had been a while since I was feeling up to going there.

Eight weeks.

That was how long I'd made it without sex. I was like a

115

dog in heat, humping my husband's legs. I hated the wait time after delivery. For the first few weeks, I didn't notice all that much. I was sore and tired and up all night with my babies.

But I was ready to fuck my husbands.

After the boys drifted to sleep, Luca set the book down on the table beside him. He rose from the couch with a sleeping Angelo. I could already see Luca bonding with Angelo, even though Leo was the oldest by three minutes.

Bastian took Leo from my arms, and Marcello extended his hand to help me up from the couch. My husbands worked so well as a team. Each night, we put our children to bed together. No matter how busy they were with their businesses, they always found time.

After the boys were in their cribs, we followed Damian to Sofia's room. She curled her little fingers around Damian's finger, eyes closed. A smile touched her lips like she knew Daddy was there with her. Damian grinned so wide I thought his face would freeze like that.

We closed Sofia's door and walked toward the stairs.

I glanced at Luca, who wove his fingers between mine. "Are you still going to honor the deal we made?"

He bobbed his head. "Of course. I want to make all of your fantasies come true."

I lifted an eyebrow at him. "All of them?"

Luca snickered. "Well, maybe not all of them." His gaze drifted to my other husbands. "You'll have to get that from Damian and Bastian. That's one line I'm not crossing."

Marcello nodded in agreement.

All of us had been dying for tonight. It felt like an eternity since we were together.

Luca and Marcello agreed to share me.

At the same time.

Marcello was down with almost anything, but not Luca. Maybe it was all the waiting fucking with his head. But when I told him it was my darkest fantasy, he said it would come true.

The Mansion. This place held so many good and bad memories. We hadn't been back since we had to tunnel our way out. But I would never forget the night my men took my virginity.

On occasion, they would reenact that night for me. Although, after years of being with them, I knew each of their bodies.

I could tell them apart in the dark.

We skipped the live shows and went straight to the penthouse apartment on the top floor. It was our private suite, untouched by other guests.

Marcello moved behind me and unzipped my dress, sliding the straps down my shoulders. I didn't bother to wear underwear.

Marcello took a moment to gaze at my naked body. "You're so beautiful." He cupped my cheek and smiled. Then his hands wandered down my sides as he placed kisses across my jaw. "I missed you, princess." His hand dipped between my thighs. "I can't wait to be inside you."

I tilted my head to the side to give him better access. "I hope you get me pregnant tonight."

He sucked my bottom lip into his mouth. "Me too."

That was the deal.

His brothers had to pull out and were all okay with it. Even Luca didn't protest.

He owed Marcello.

They all did.

My other husbands were anxious to get their hands on me and yanked me away from Marcello. Damian pushed my back to the mattress, and with Bastian's help, they spread my thighs.

"My sweet cherry," Bastian grunted, with his eyes between my legs as Damian rubbed his thumb over my clit.

"My Pet is so wet for me." He plunged his finger into me, adding another and increasing his pace. His head lifted to look at Bastian. "For us."

Luca and Marcello got onto the bed.

"My queen." Luca's voice was deep and smooth. "We're going to devour you."

Marcello bent down to suck my nipple into his mouth, ripping a squeal from me. Then Bastian's lips were on my inner thigh, Damian planting even hotter kisses on my pussy. Warmth spread throughout my body, my skin sizzling from the intense toe-curling sensation.

My sexy hunters lifted their heads and stared at me with their lips parted and glistening with my cum. They took turns tasting me, their tongues brushing with each flick.

Luca sat up, taking me with him. "I'm done waiting." He pointed at the mattress and tipped his head for Marcello to lay on his back. "Time to bring your fantasy to life, Mrs. Salvatore."

I climbed on top of Marcello, and Luca got behind me.

And then the lights went out.

I was used to the dark and no longer feared it. My men lived in it and taught me how to thrive.

Luca gripped my hip from behind, and his lips moved up and down my neck.

His brothers touched every inch of my body. Even in the dark, I knew Damian was on my right. Bastian was on my left. Their big hands brushed my legs and breasts. My nipples were so sensitive when their thumbs rolled over the tiny buds.

I sat up and pushed Marcello inside me, rocking my hips as my husbands worshiped me. Luca put his hand on my shoulder, breathing in my ear. I could feel the hesitation in his movements as he lubed his cock, then my entrance.

"Luca," I moaned. "Fuck me. Please."

With his hand on my back, he pushed into me, taking his time. A hiss escaped his throat.

"Fuck," he groaned. "And I thought your pussy was tight."

I palmed Marcello's chest to brace myself, and Damian clutched my arm to steady me. It had been too long since I had two men inside me.

I missed it.

With Bastian and Damian kneeling at my sides, I traced my fingers over their chests and arms. Luca nibbled on my ear and fucked me without mercy. He didn't think he would like anal.

I proved him wrong.

As usual.

Damian's woodsy scent filled my nostrils when he leaned over to kiss my neck. "You're such a good girl, Pet." He flicked his tongue on my lip. "I'm going to fuck all of your pretty holes."

"Mmm," I whimpered. "I want that."

Luca leaned forward and bit my earlobe. "Scream my name, baby girl."

I moaned each of their names as I came. Marcello etched his fingers into my hips, his thrusts getting more aggressive as he raced to the finish line with me.

Damian rubbed my clit as Bastian sucked on my nipple. My men had the perfect rhythm.

Marcello was the first to come.

Luca pulled out, his cum splashing my ass. "Fucking hell," he grunted. "I don't think I've ever come like that before."

"See," I said with a smile he couldn't see in the dark. "I told you this would be fun."

"Stop denying yourself pleasure." Bastian tapped Luca's arm. "It's time to let go."

Luca snickered. "I just did."

There was no point in arguing with Luca. This was a big

step for him, something I never thought he would do. He liked to stay in his comfort zone.

Damian lifted me off Marcello and put me on my knees, quickly entering me from behind. "You're so wet, Pet." He was a madman, driving into me like he was losing control. "It's been too long. Fuck."

He fucked me for what felt like hours before he pulled out and pushed me onto my back. After that, it was Bash's turn to make me scream. And then Damian was behind Bastian.

Damian came before Bastian, grunting our names. And when Bastian was about to come, he pulled out, coating my stomach and breasts with his cum.

Luca got off the bed and grabbed a warm towel. He cleaned me up and kissed my lips. "You're perfect, Drea."

Marcello and Bastian grunted in agreement.

Damian dropped to the bed beside me. "Perfect for us."

Chapter Twenty

ALEX

Marcello's birthday was one week before Christmas. Instead of doing something fun, he wanted to sit in the living room and wrap presents. He was in Dad Mode, cutting paper for the kids presents with precision. When he was in the zone, he looked so serious and determined.

So damn cute.

Bastian was beside us, helping Damian wrap a diamond tiara for Sofia. He had it designed by a jeweler in Italy to fit our baby girl's little head. We'd be lucky if we could take one picture of her wearing it before it ended up on the floor.

"No, D," Bastian groaned, tugging on the paper. "Like this. When are you going to learn how to wrap a fucking present?" He shook his head. "You can speak several languages fluently, but you can't fold a piece of paper and put tape on it?"

Damian elbowed him, a smirk in place. "Why bother learning when I know you'll do it for me?"

Bastian dropped the tape on the floor. "You're an asshole."

I gave them my best angry face. "No fighting, husbands."

"We're not fighting," Bastian countered.

"You two have been at each other's throats lately."

"It's just stress, Cherry." Bastian got up from the floor and extended his hand to Damian as a peace offering. "Atlantic Airlines is going through a lot of changes."

Damian took his hand and rose to his full height. "We've been together a long time." He slid his arm across Bastian's back, resting his hand on his hip. "It's nothing serious, Pet."

They were buying two smaller airlines and absorbing them into Atlantic Airlines. I knew nothing about running a company, but it sounded stressful. And I could tell by the dark circles under Bastian's eyes that he was lying about getting the proper amount of sleep.

I stood between my three husbands, who circled me. "It's Marcello's special day. Be nice to each other."

Marcello chuckled. "There's nothing special about my birthday, princess."

I stood on my tiptoes and hooked my arms around his neck. "Your twenty-fifth birthday is special to me. I got you something to celebrate."

He was eighteen months younger than Luca. I often teased him that I was robbing the cradle.

"I told you no presents." He kissed my lips, and his hands rested on my hips. "I already have everything I want."

My lips brushed his. "I'm not your present."

"You're the only thing I want." Marcello's grip tightened around me. "I couldn't ask for a better gift."

A smile tugged at the corners of my mouth. "Well, I didn't pay for your present if it makes you feel better. I painted it."

"Oh." His eyebrows rose in curiosity. "Let me see it."

He loved when I surprised him with art. So technically, I stuck to the no-present rule.

I slipped out of Marcello's grasp and poked my head into the hallway. Luca left the room a few minutes ago to grab a box of cigars from his study and was on his way back.

I raised my hand and waved Luca forward. "Hurry up."

He strolled down the hallway with his usual swagger, the

wooden box tucked under his arm. "I'm coming, woman. Calm down."

"Don't tell your queen to calm down, Mr. Salvatore."

Luca's dress shoes slapped the marble floor as he approached me. Smirking, he lifted my feet off the ground and carried me into the room. "How about I spank you for talking back, Mrs. Salvatore?"

"Don't tease me." I flicked my tongue over his earlobe. "I could use a good spanking."

"I'll get the rope," Bastian offered.

"Not now," Luca shot back. "Save that for later."

This wasn't the time to think about sex. Or was it? Whenever I was with my husbands, they made it impossible not to think about all the dirty ways they claimed my body.

Luca set me down and tipped his head at the canvas I wrapped in our bedroom last night. He lay on the bed beside me with the twins' heads rested on his chest.

It was adorable.

Daddy and his boys.

So I snapped a few pictures. I wanted the capture that moment for a future painting. My men inspired a lot of my work. And lately, the kids were popping up in a new series I had yet to reveal to the world.

I handed Marcello the painting, and he pulled me to the couch beside him. I sucked in a deep breath as he tore off the paper. His gaze shifted from the woman on the canvas, those pretty blue eyes holding mine.

A painting of me.

In my typical modern Art Deco style, I wore a sleek black dress, a string of pearls, and held a pregnancy test in my hand.

It had two blue lines.

I wrote the date at the bottom, so we would never forget this day. I started the painting a few months ago to give it to Marcello. But until this morning, I didn't know I was pregnant.

"You're pregnant?" Marcello's smile lit up his handsome face. "The baby is mine?"

I nodded. "Your brothers have kept their promise."

"I've been pulling out minutes before I come," Bastian told him.

"Same," Luca added.

Damian sat beside me and grabbed my backside. "And I've only been fucking her sweet ass."

"This is your child, Marcello."

I launched myself into his arms, and he hugged me, sniffing on my shoulder. He kept his head there until he regained his emotions. And when our gazes met, his eyes were glassy.

His fingers slipped through my hair, a smile on his handsome face. "This is number one."

Bastian kicked his feet on the ottoman and leaned back, arms crossed over his chest. "What are you talking about?"

"Before Marcello left for his last mission, I wanted to hear something good to cheer me up. He said our first kiss was one of the best days of his life. I asked him what number one was, and he said we hadn't reached it yet because he hadn't gotten me pregnant."

"Ooh, I wanna play," Bash said with laughter in his tone. "When you told me you loved me at The Mansion. That was one of mine."

Damian leaned over and put his arm across the back of my neck. "The day you gave me Sofia. Also the first time we had sex, and you forced me to kiss you."

"You were so against kissing." I tugged on his shirt and brought his lips to mine. "Look at you now. You're always kissing me."

"Our wedding day." Luca studied my face and smiled. "The day the twins were born."

"They were amazing days," I agreed.

"When you said you loved me, even though you thought I

was sleeping." Luca's intense blue eyes met mine. "But one day that stands out is when you explained my mother's fresco to me. I knew I loved you right then and there. It just took me a long time to say it."

I turned to look at Marcello when he yanked me away from Damian with possession. "I have a lot of favorite moments with you, princess. But my top five are our first kiss and the first time we painted together. When you told me you would choose me over Luca."

"Not the fucking highlight of my life," Luca shot back, shaking his head. "Dickhead."

"Don't be a hater," Marcello said with laughter dripping from his tone. "I won fair and square, and you know it."

Luca smirked. "My name is on the marriage license. So the best man still won."

"Hey." I snapped my fingers at Luca. "Knock that off. It's Marcello's birthday. You're not ruining it by being a grouch."

"I'm simply pointing out a basic truth," Luca said in his defense. "You're my wife on paper."

"And I'm divorcing you and marrying Marcello if you don't stop throwing it in his face."

"Oh, shit." Bastian slapped his thigh and laughed. "I'd like to see that."

Luca warned his brother with an intense look that set my skin on fire. A moment of silence ensued where Luca lifted the cigar box and tossed Cubans to his brothers to diffuse the situation.

Marcello and Luca were closer than ever, but they still had their moments. Time would not change Luca. Not even I could make him become a completely different man. But this was a vast improvement, and I loved how much he'd grown over the years.

Marcello tucked the cigar behind his ear. Luca lounged beside Bastian in the armchair and cut the cigar's tip.

"I'm not done with my list." Damian moved close enough

125

that I could feel his breath on my earlobe. "Your first day at Astor Prep makes my top ten. And then, there's the day you said you love me in the dining room. I didn't think I would ever be worthy of your love. But you showed me I was wrong."

I flipped my hair over my shoulder and smiled. "I'm usually right about matters of the heart."

"The day I learned I would be a dad is another one. Even if I didn't act like I was happy at first." He pressed his finger to his blood-red lips. "I only got one of your firsts, but you had almost all of mine."

Bastian interrupted our sweet moment with his confession. "Taking your virginity is in the top five for me." He blew out a plume of cigar smoke that gathered around his head. "When the first note of your song came to me, I'd never felt so inspired. I can't write anymore without my muse."

I sat between Marcello and Damian, each claiming a thigh.

"All of your favorite moments are mine, too," I admitted. "I love you. And I love our life together. I couldn't imagine doing this without each of you. No more fighting, please. I know you guys are all under a lot of stress, but Christmas is next week. This is supposed to be the happiest time of the year."

"We didn't mean to upset you, Cherry." Bastian stamped out his cigar in the ashtray and stood, looking so damn tall as he strolled over to me. "Sometimes, families disagree." He kneeled between my thighs and placed his hand on my knee. "But we love each other. And we love you. This is going to be the best Christmas you ever had."

Marcello reached over to rub my stomach, even though I couldn't have been more than a month along and wasn't showing.

A smile touched my lips. "We're going to have a big family."

"Which means a lot of fighting," Luca said as he moved behind Bastian, staring down at me. "It's bound to happen, baby. But Bash is right." He tapped his brother's shoulder. "This is going to be a Christmas you'll never forget."

My right eyebrow lifted at his confession. "How so?"

Luca grinned like an evil mastermind. "You'll see."

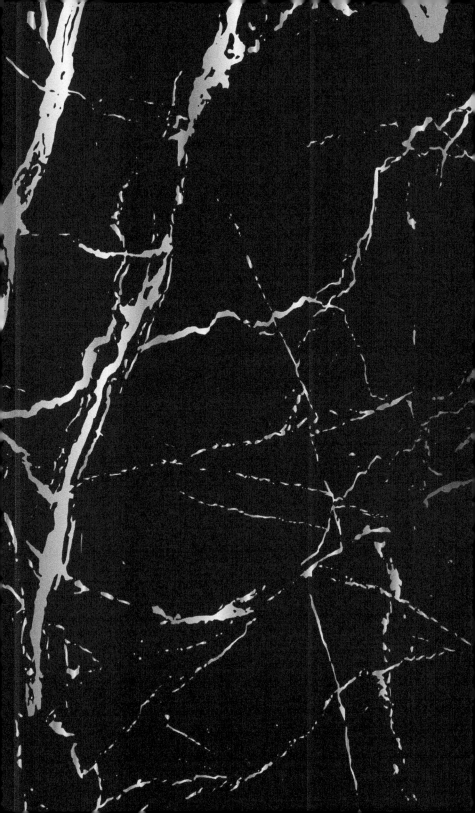

PART TWO

THE SALVATORE LEGACY

Chapter Twenty-One

DAMIAN

Nine years later...

A scream woke me from a dreamless sleep. I patted the space beside me and remembered Alex was with Luca tonight. Another panicked, high-pitched scream came from across the hall.

Sofia.

I rushed out of my bedroom and opened Sofia's door. A nightlight bathed the room in a golden glow of stars that floated across the ceiling. The Swan Lake mural Marcello had painted of Odette was on the opposite wall, right in front of Sofia's toys. She was so spoiled. My baby girl had everything she could ever want.

She sat in the middle of her bed. "Daddy," she choked out with tears in her eyes, relief washing over her face.

I sat on the bed and cradled her head against my chest. "Did you have another bad dream, princess?"

She bobbed her head, still crying. "The monsters came back again."

I ran my fingers through her long, sweaty black hair, down her back, which was also slick with sweat, her pajamas clinging to her tiny body. "It's okay now. Daddy's here. The monsters are afraid of me."

She didn't know how true that was, but she believed it. Because she thought her dad was invincible.

I wasn't.

Just a crazy motherfucker who would kill anyone or anything that tried to fuck with my family. And with Sofia, I was even more of a savage.

Sofia was ten, not much older than me when I started having nightmares.

"Daddy, will you tell me a story?" Sofia peeked up at me with her mother's big blue eyes.

She looked like my mom when she was a child, but with just enough of Alex, you could see the similarities. Even if we didn't take a paternity test, I would have known Sofia was mine.

I tucked her sweaty hair behind her ears and smiled. "Lie back down. I'll get in with you."

She did as I asked and curled up on her side, staring at me as I got in the bed with her. I always stayed with her until after she fell asleep on the nights she had bad dreams. Some nights, I even passed out beside her.

The day she was born, I felt even more possessive than I had felt with Alex. Of course, I would have died for my wife, done anything to protect her. But there was something different about my bond with Sofia. It was unlike anything I had with Alex or my brothers. She wasn't just my family.

She was my blood.

Mine.

I'd had nothing to call my own until she came into this world. Alex gave me a gift I never thought I was worthy to receive. And now that I had Sofia, I would do anything for her. Be anything she needed. Her dad, her best friend, whatever she wanted me to be.

She placed her tiny hand on top of mine and closed her

eyes. There was so much darkness inside me it tainted my heart black.

This precious little girl saved me.

I still wasn't entirely sane, and occasionally, I had to kill to protect my family, but I no longer felt the bloodlust. I imagined what Sofia would think if she knew I almost killed her mother by accident.

"Once upon a time," I said in a hushed tone, "there was a princess named Sofia."

"Daddy." She giggled. "Why do all the princesses have the same name as me?"

"Because all princesses are called Sofia."

"No, they're not!" She laughed again. "You're so silly, Daddy."

I brushed her cheek with the pad of my thumb. "Do you want to hear the story or not?"

"Yes." She smiled up at me like I hung the moon. "I want dragons in this story."

I grinned like a fucking idiot because this little girl always put a smile on my face. Before she was born, I never smiled unless Alex ripped one out of me.

"There once was a princess named Sofia," I told her. "She lived in a great big castle on the sea with four knights and a powerful queen."

She nestled her face against the pillow and laughed. "Why is Mommy always the queen?"

"Who says it's her?"

"I have four daddies and one mommy."

Sofia was too young to understand our unconventional relationship. Her friends asked a lot of questions. Why does Daddy Damian take you to school and Daddy Marcello pick you up? Not to mention when people saw the five of us in public with our children. It was clear we were with Alex.

"That makes you even more special than other kids." I traced my fingers down her arm. "You have four knights to protect you and a queen who will do anything to keep you safe."

After that, she let me tell the story and passed out beside me. I almost dozed off until I heard the door creak, and the light from the hallway filled the dark room.

Alex stood in the entryway, with her hand on the door-knob, a big smile on her face.

Careful not to disturb Sofia, I took one last look at her and followed Alex into the hallway, closing the door behind me.

I gripped her hip, pushing up the silk top, showing off her toned stomach. After having five children, she still looked incredible. Her body filled out with curves, and her breasts were even bigger.

"Everything okay, Pet?"

She smiled, standing on her tippy toes to kiss me. "I love seeing you with Sofia. You're such a good dad, Damian."

In most areas of my life, I needed reassurance that I was doing the right thing—someone to tell me if my behavior was normal. But with Sofia, I never had to ask myself that question. I knew I was a good dad. And I loved when Alex confirmed that, making me believe it even more.

I kissed her back. "Sofia had another nightmare."

Alex pushed on my chest until my back hit the wall. Hooking her leg around me, she rubbed her pussy on my cock. "I want to make more babies with you."

She'd been like this since Cato turned five. Bastian was the last of us to get Alex pregnant, and Cato was supposed to be the last pregnancy. But she enjoyed being pregnant and having our babies.

My dick poked through the slit in my boxers, teasing her wetness through her shorts. I stripped off her bottoms and lifted her into my arms. Using the wall as an anchor, I leaned back and rocked into her.

Her head fell to my chest, and she breathed on my neck. "Damian."

I wanted to fuck her good, so I carried her down the hall and into my bedroom. Without breaking our bond, I lowered us to the bed and continued to thrust deeper, ripping screams from her beautiful lips. She grabbed my hand and wrapped it around her throat. My girl loved when I put my mark on her.

Made her mine.

"Tie me up, Damian."

I smiled at her request. "Bad, Pet."

I lifted one of the red silk straps attached to the bedpost. I pinned Alex's arms above her head and secured her wrists one at a time. Thrusting into her harder, she whimpered each time, squeezing my cock with her pussy.

"You're so wet," I grunted, breathing through my nose. "Fuck, you feel good."

"So do you." Her eyes locked onto mine. "Harder, Damian. Let your brothers see every place you touched me."

A sick grin tugged at my mouth.

Alex said I wrecked her pussy every time we fucked. I changed a lot over the years but still enjoyed rough sex. If she wanted slow and sweet, she went to Marcello or Bastian.

They could give that to her.

Even Luca had his moments where he was a different man with her. But Alex didn't come to me to make love. She wanted me to fuck her so hard and fast she couldn't catch her breath. My wife wanted me to shatter her existence with each orgasm.

So I gave it to her.

My eyes dropped to her breasts. Over her heart, she had a tattoo that said *Pet*. In the exact spot where I had her name.

With Alex on her back, I couldn't see the two cherries she got behind her ear for Bastian. Or the ink she got for Luca— Drea written in script on her neck. She had a princess tiara above her right shoulder blade for Marcello.

A few months after she delivered Cato, we went to the tattoo studio where Aiden got his ink. Alex was never into tattoos, not even after she'd spent years admiring my work. She decided it was time to get something more permanent for our tenth wedding anniversary, a physical reminder of our love.

"Oh, God, Damian," Alex moaned.

Thankfully, this house had thick walls and doors. The kids' rooms were on the other side of the hall from mine. Alex licked her lips, legs wrapped around me, encouraging me to fuck her harder.

"You're an animal," she whimpered. "Fuck."

She rocked her hips, greedy for more. So I held her down, each thrust harder than the last. It didn't take long before a tremor rocked through her body, and she begged me for more as the orgasm swept over her.

I was right there with her, so close my legs shook. Slowing my pace, I curled my fingers around her throat to send both of us over the edge. The first time I applied this much pressure, she flipped out. I didn't blame her for not trusting me back then, not when I almost killed her.

Now, we had a comfortable rhythm. Alex trusted me to take her to the brink of madness. I could control my urges and knew my limits.

After we both came, I pulled out and released her from the ties holding her arms in place. Years of Bastian practicing Kinbaku and Shibari on Alex made her feel comfortable tied up. She could sit in one place for hours while he tried different bondage techniques on her.

I moved between her spread thighs and kissed her wet pussy, licking her straight down the center. She was usually sore after we had sex but loved the pain.

We both got off on it.

I sucked her clit into my mouth.

She hissed.

"Did I fuck you too hard?"

"No," she whispered. "It feels good. Don't stop."

I spread her thighs wider and kissed her soft skin. She ran her fingers through my hair and tugged at the ends. When her legs trembled, I pinned her to the mattress, licking and sucking until another orgasm commanded her body.

She struggled to catch her breath, holding her hand over her rapidly beating heart.

I inched up her body, one kiss at a time, until I reached her mouth.

"How come you're not with Luca?"

"He got a call around midnight. The Sicilians needed his help mapping new trade routes."

That was not my area of expertise. Luca was good at figuring out all the loopholes for our criminal counterparts.

"I came downstairs to check on the kids." She smiled. "I found Cato in bed with Bash. Eve was snoring softly in her room. Leo and Angelo fell asleep on the floor next to their chess set." She shook her head. "Luca has rubbed off on them so much. They're like mini versions of him."

"By design," I told her. "Luca is making sure they understand their role in this family. One of them will take over for him someday."

"Yeah." She sighed. "But they're still my babies."

"They're nine," I pointed out. "We were like grown men by the time we were their age."

"Trauma aged all of you much faster. But the twins don't have that kind of life. They have four dads, a mom, aunts, uncles, and grandfathers who love them. Our kids will never have to grow up the way we did."

I kissed her lips, and she melted in my arms. "Our kids will never have a normal life, but the next generation of Knights will be different."

"I worry about them going through the Knights' initiation." She bit her lip. "Sofia and Eve can do anything they want. So can Cato. They don't have the same obligations."

"Cato will be a Knight, too. But not the leader."

Cato was five years old and a long way from us thinking about him becoming a Knight. Lately, Alex had been so worried about the boys. She knew the girls would have the freedom to do whatever they wanted. But our boys would be Knights, and one twin would be the new Grand Master.

She frowned. "I don't want my boys hardened by this world."

"They won't be anything like us," I assured her.

"Leo and Angelo are already like Luca."

"He's preparing them."

"But they're little boys," she groaned. "They don't need to be chess masters before they hit puberty. I'd rather see them playing with their friends and doing normal boy things."

"We didn't do any of those things. Our dad never let us play with other kids. It was always the four of us against the world. Luca is just doing what he knows."

"Yeah, but Sofia and Eve have friends. They go on play-dates with the girls from school."

Eve was Marcello's little girl, named after his mother, Evangeline. Except our girl was just Eve. She was born a year after the twins and was almost seven years old. And she was learning how to paint on canvases, like her mother and father.

Years ago, I never thought I would be the person Alex confided in. I wasn't mentally in the right place to give advice. But over the years, I had been her sounding board. I listened and let her talk. I told her the truth when she needed to hear it.

Marcello told her whatever he thought she wanted to hear. He was such a fucking softie. Bash spoke the truth but sugar-coated everything. Luca was blunt, which led to a lot of fights. He would grovel and beg for forgiveness afterward. But he was still the same asshole.

She told me everything—all of her desires, fears, every-thing that was on her mind.

"I love you." I slipped my fingers through her hair and

kissed her lips. "And because I love you, I won't lie to you. The twins will be exactly like Luca, and it will serve them well. Salvatore men are not weak. We don't cower. People in our world need to fear the Salvatore name."

She laid her head on my chest. "I feel like I'm losing time with the boys. They're growing up so fast. Even Sofia is like a little woman already."

I laughed. "Not quite. Our little girl still clings to her daddy and wants to hear princess stories. Sofia is still your baby."

She rubbed her hand over her stomach. "I'm ovulating. I hope you put another baby in me."

"We'll try until you get pregnant again." I sucked her bottom lip into my mouth. "I love making babies with you."

She tugged at the ends of my short hair and smiled. "Of all my husbands, you surprised me the most."

"Happy to exceed expectations."

Chapter Twenty-Two

BASTIAN

Three years later...

"Cato Severus Salvatore," I shouted at my son, who tore apart the backyard like a lunatic. "Get over here." I patted my thigh, giving him my best angry face. "Let's go. Now!"

Cato was such a devious little bastard. And here I thought Damian's kid would be the devil spawn of the family. But, nope, my little terror was the worst of the Salvatore clan.

I wasn't mad, just not in the mood to deal with his games today. He was like a golden retriever puppy, always getting into everything. Whenever Luca was around, Cato stood ramrod straight, eyes wide. Luca was mean, more demanding than all of us, but he was a good dad.

Maybe I was too soft with Cato.

He was mine, and I loved that kid more than life. I let him get away with murder because he was so damn cute. And so bright, which was why he was always in trouble. He thought he knew better than everyone else.

Cato strolled to me with the mallet dragging behind him,

frowning. He had my brown hair that was always messy and falling onto his forehead, styled like Daddy Marcello.

He'd taken to Marcello as if he were his father and wanted to dress like him. It annoyed me because I wanted him to be like me, but all five kids were ours. So the paternity didn't matter.

When I tried teaching Cato how to play the piano, he slammed his hands down on the keys and tried to walk across them. A million-dollar Steinway & Sons grand piano.

This fucking kid was the devil.

"What did I tell you about beating the grass with the mallet?" I pushed the hair out of his gray eyes and held back an irritated scowl. "You put dozens of holes in the grass. Daddy Luca will beat your butt if you don't knock that off."

Luca still had zero tolerance for bullshit. He was usually the disciplinarian, and his voice alone was enough to get them to follow the rules. He never hit them, only threatened to do it. That alone was enough to keep them all in line.

The girls were easy.

They went with the flow and never gave us shit. Eve and Sofia were two years apart and were best friends. They did everything together, except for paint. While Eve followed in her mother's footsteps and loved to paint, Sofia was more like Damian.

He taught her how to fish and hunt. At thirteen, she was the oldest and had just started archery lessons. She was like a little Arya Stark. Eve was creative and a free spirit like her mother, always with paint on her clothes and hair.

"Sorry, Dad," Cato groaned. "But how do you expect me to play croquet without making divots?"

Our kids were bougie like that. Instead of playing with Nerf balls and water guns, they wanted to learn croquet and golf and take archery lessons and weird-ass shit normal kids didn't do.

That was all Luca.

He was an elitist snob.

I extended my hand. "Give me the mallet. I'll show you."

He threw it at my feet and crossed his arms over his chest.

"You better pick that up, Cato." I pointed at it. "Now!"

He was eight and still acting like he was going through the terrible twos.

"Cato," Alex said in a singsong voice. "Come here, baby. Look what Momma got you."

All the kids called Alex something different. She was Momma to Cato. Ma to Leo, Angelo, and Eve. Mommy to Sofia.

Cato rushed past me and snickered like he'd won a match. *Damn kid.*

He launched himself into Alex's arms, so the queen could protect him from the mean knight who wanted him to behave. Alex lifted him off the ground, even though she struggled to pick him up. She was pregnant again after trying for the past three years. We weren't getting any younger, and the doctor said it would be more challenging now that we were all closer to forty.

Her belly was too round to carry an eight-year-old baby on her hip. But Cato climbed her like a tree. He loved the shit out of his mom. Whenever she walked into a room, his face lit up. Just the sound of her voice had him running toward her.

"You're going to hurt Momma." I gripped his shoulder. "Get down."

"It's okay, Bash." Alex shifted him on her hip. "He's still my baby." She kissed his sweaty forehead, and he smiled as she gave him the popsicle in her hand. "Here, eat before Daddy Luca sees."

Luca only let the kids have sugar on rare occasions. He was a possessive control freak, even with the kids and their schedules. As he did with Alex, he picked out their clothes, planned their lives down to the second, and even tried to do that shit with us.

After Cato ate half of the cherry popsicle, Alex set him on the ground. He ran toward the swing set in the backyard, dripping red juice all over the lawn.

"Why does that kid hate me so much?" I shoved a hand through my hair and sighed. "It's like the more I try to connect with him, the more he pushes me away."

Alex stood on her tippy toes and hooked her arms around my neck. She wore a red sundress that made her blonde hair look even more golden. "Cato is going through a phase. He'll bond with you. Give it time."

I shook my head. "No, he won't. He already did that with Marcello."

She took my hand and placed it on her stomach, moving our joined hands in a circular motion. "This child is yours, Bash. You'll get another chance with him. Cato doesn't hate you. He doesn't fear you like he does your brothers."

"So I'm supposed to be an asshole to make him like me?"

"You're different with Cato," she said softly as her eyes wandered over to the playground where Cato stood on the swing instead of sitting on it. "It seems like you're disappointed that he's not like you."

"I'm not. I love that kid to death. I would do anything for him." I threw out my hand at our son. "But look at him. It's like he's missing a few screws. None of our other kids stand on swings or grand pianos. They don't intentionally put holes in the lawn and spill paint on marble floors to put their footprints in them."

"He's special." She grinned. "Cato needs more love than the other kids. So spend more time with him. Try to teach him something he likes."

"I've tried."

"He doesn't like the piano, Bash." She threaded her fingers between mine. "You can't force your passions on him. I taught him to paint and look what he did. Paint all over every surface of the house."

"I thought Luca was going to kill him."

She giggled. "That's what he does when he's bored."

"Because he has screws loose," I quipped. "Are you sure he's not Damian's?"

She laughed so hard it shook through me. "He's yours. You heard what the doctor said. She thinks he might be a genius. Cato gets bored and acts out."

"That kid is smart, but I don't know about a genius."

"His dad is a prodigy pianist. I'd say it runs in his genes." As she moved our hands over her belly, our son kicked. "Did you feel that?"

I smiled. "I love feeling him move around."

"You try getting kicked in the stomach. It's not fun."

"Cato punched me in the dick last week. So yeah, I kinda feel your pain."

"Who taught him that?" She tilted her head to the side and looked up at me. "He's been doing that to you a lot lately."

"One of my asshole brothers. And if I find out which one, I will kill him."

"I can't let you kill my husbands."

I tightened my grip on her, tapping my fingers on her hip. "I bet it was Marcello. He showed that move to Sofia after that little shit at her school tried to kiss her."

"I can't believe she's thirteen already." Alex breathed through her nose, eyes across the yard on Cato, who jumped from the top of the jungle gym. "Our babies are growing too fast."

"You'll have a new one to baby all over again." I rubbed her stomach. "I think you just like being pregnant."

She chuckled. "Sofia is almost in high school. Angelo and Leo are like grown men. Pretty soon, Eve will have her first art show. And Cato…"

"My sweet cherry," I said against the shell of her ear.

"They're still kids. Eve has another eight years before she can even apply to art school."

"What do you want to name him?" Our son kicked again, and she winced. "We need to decide soon. He'll be here any day."

"How about another Roman name?"

"Hmmm…" Deep in thought, she put her index finger in front of her lips. "How about Marcus for your biological father?"

Alex found ways to honor each of our parents. Eve for Evangeline and Sofia for Damian's mom. She didn't want us to lose the people who shaped our lives, and I loved her even more for it.

We all did.

I kissed the top of her head. "Marcus is perfect."

Alex let me choose Cato's name, which came from Marcus Porcius Cato, the Roman senator. So Marcus fit for our second child together.

"You're a good dad," she told me. "Cato will come around. I think he sees you differently than your brothers. He knows they're not his dad biologically and doesn't treat them the same. In his mind, you're the parent. They're more like his cool uncles."

I laughed at her comment. "Technically, they are his uncles."

"Yeah, sure. But that's not how we're raising them. You are just as much the father of Eve as Marcello. These kids are so lucky to have four dads. Most people don't get one decent dad."

I kissed the cherry tattoo she'd gotten behind her right ear, sucking the lobe into my mouth.

After the kids were born, she got a tattoo to represent each of us. We each took turns kissing her in the places we marked. Showing her how much we loved and worshiped her.

Even after nearly fifteen years, we still fucked her together every week. None of us were too busy to find time to be together.

Alex moved between each of our beds every night. We preferred it that way and had no plans to change our routine. But on Saturdays, the kids spent time with our relatives, so we could claim every inch of our wife's body. Over and over for twenty-four hours straight.

"I love you, Cherry." I dragged my tongue across her ear, and she whimpered. "You're the best thing that ever happened to us."

"Duh." Alex chuckled. "But you guys were a godsend. And to think I wanted to run when you made me come back to Devil's Creek."

"I'm glad you didn't run." I turned her head to the side to kiss her pretty pink lips. "Even if you did, we would have chased you to the ends of the earth."

Chapter Twenty-Three

MARCELLO

Two years later...

At least two hundred people gathered at the Franco-Salvatore Gallery, a converted warehouse in Devil's Creek. Alex opened the gallery with Luca's help five years ago. The surprise anniversary gift would have been from all of us if the bastard had told us about it.

Luca still liked to play games.

Anything to make us look bad.

Alex was his wife on paper, and he ensured we remembered that.

But she was ours.

So, it surprised me when he asked for our help with this event to celebrate the next generation.

Years ago, Alex had turned the art world upside down with her modern Art Deco underworld-inspired paintings. She was still the Franco Foundation director, the gallery curator, and a solo artist. And the mother of six beautiful children, with the seventh on the way.

Lucky number seven.

This time, Alex didn't want to know the sex or the paternity. So it would be a surprise to discover in the birthing room.

Luca and Bastian each had two boys.

Damian stood in front of one of Alex's paintings beside Sofia. She was fifteen and a sophomore in high school.

Sofia looked exactly like Damian, with long black hair and her mother's big blue eyes. She was beautiful, drawing way too much attention from the boys at Astor Prep.

Thankfully, Leo and Angelo were as intimidating as Luca in their first year. According to Sofia, they terrorized everyone at school and kept the boys away from her. I could only imagine the mini versions of Luca running around that school like my brother did during his reign of terror.

Eve was thirteen and had been painting since she was seven. Back then, it was just for fun—a splash of color on a canvas, a few lines, and swirls. But my little girl was becoming a real artist.

I held her trembling hand and steered her over to the paintings displayed on the wall. Canvases both of us painted for the show. "It's okay to be nervous," I told her. "But you don't have to be. You're so talented, Eve."

She peeked up at me and smiled. "What if people think I suck? I'm not as good as Ma or Nonna."

Even though she'd never met my mom, she still called her Nonna. We talked about her as if she were still here. And after Eve started painting, she wanted to study my mother's work. She said her art spoke to her, just like Alex had said years ago.

They were so much alike.

The perfect mother-daughter team.

"You're just as talented, Eve." I rubbed her back with my palm and traced soothing circles to calm her nerves. "Age means nothing in the art world."

"But Ma is a natural. She started sketching when she was two."

"While your friends painted with their fingers, you were

creating art." I kissed the top of her head. "I love you. We all do. I'm so proud of you. And I can guarantee everyone will love your paintings."

Luca was on the other side of the room, with Leo and Angelo clinging to his sides. We used to follow our father around the same way. The boys worshiped Luca and thought he was the king of the world.

Alex stood beside Bastian with a two-year-old Marcus on her hip and a ten-year-old Cato between them. He bent down, kissed her cheek, and planted a kiss on Marcus's head.

Initially, Cato was my shadow and followed me around the house. But after Alex had Marcus, Bash finally found some common ground. Cato was a prodigy like Bash, gifted in math and science. The doctors suspected Cato had ADHD because he quickly got bored doing everyday kid things and acted out.

With the help of his dad, Cato developed a music app and got it approved in the app store after working on it for the past year.

As I watched them from a distance, I couldn't help but smile. We all felt bad for Bash for the longest time. He was the only one who couldn't bond with his kid.

I tapped Eve's shoulder when Alex raised her hand and waved us over. "It's time to go, *bambina*."

Alex wanted to introduce all the artists in the family. She even convinced me to add a few paintings to the exhibit. Of course, Eve couldn't wait to paint something to honor Nonna. But now that people surrounded her, she was biting her nails and fidgeting. Even with me at her side, trying to comfort her, I could see the worry lines pulling at her forehead.

She was so much like her mother.

Intelligent and beautiful, so intuitive and creative. A bit of a free spirit, too. But she never enjoyed being around many people. With eleven of us living under the same roof and another baby on the way, she still hadn't gotten used to crowds. My girl was a lot like me in that way. I never liked the attention our family attracted.

Luca wanted to be feared, admired and loved for his accomplishments. I preferred to remain in the shadows and let him lead our family. Eve had a lot of me in her. Maybe it was from observing me, noticing how uncomfortable I was in social settings.

Alex stood on the stage with a microphone in hand. Luca was beside her with our kids behind them. In public, we had to act like our children were Luca's, even though most people in town gossiped and made assumptions.

You could tell Sofia was Damian's daughter. Even with Alex's big blue eyes, she looked like her father. Same with Cato. He had Bash's brown hair and gray eyes and Alex's high cheekbones. Marcus was a mixture of them and still had a babyface.

Eve, Angelo, and Leo inherited the Salvatore genes. Except for Leo, who had Alex's blonde curly hair. He cut his hair short, like his uncle Aiden. But in terms of looks, the twins were the spitting image of Luca. When we were kids, people thought Luca and I were twins. So they could easily pass for my sons, too.

I walked onto the stage with Eve. My brothers gathered beside me with their kids.

Alex clutched the microphone, a smile on her face. A round of applause rang out, and she waited for the crowd to die down before she spoke.

"Thank you all for coming. As you all know, Evangeline Franco inspired my art. And as her daughter-in-law and the director of the Franco Foundation, I'm delighted to introduce two new artists. Marcello Salvatore, Evangeline's son, and my daughter, Eve."

My cheeks burned with all the attention on me. The event was for a good cause, another way for us to raise more money for charity. Knowing both of her parents were part of the showcase made Eve feel better about displaying her art to the public.

After months of the three of us putting our hearts and souls into our paintings, they hung around the room for everyone to see. I put my hand on Eve's shoulder and smiled. She returned my expression and leaned into my side.

"Thanks to all of your contributions," Alex continued, "we have raised over one hundred million dollars for a good cause." She clutched her baby bump and winced, turning her head to the side to look at Luca. "Ow."

Luca put his arm around her and lowered his head, whispering. I wanted so badly to comfort her. But there were too many people studying our every move.

My dad was in the front row with his girlfriend and our kid's nanny, Adriana. He would never remarry. As far as he was concerned, my mother was the love of his life. But at least he was happy with Adriana. She put a smile on the miserable bastard's face.

"I'm so sorry," Alex said into the microphone, breathing hard. She patted her stomach, her face twisted in pain. "I think this child is ready to come into this world."

Déjà vu.

Her water broke on the stage at the fifteenth-anniversary showcase, and she delivered Sofia later that night.

Luca took the microphone from her hand and gave it to our dad. Our family left the stage, and people applauded as we exited the room. Some even patted our backs.

"Ma stole the show," Eve said with a smile. "At least no one booed me from the stage."

I shook my head and laughed. "No one would boo you."

"And if they did, I would cut them into tiny pieces," Damian added.

"Tone it down, killer," I shot back.

He shrugged. "What? I would. No one messes with our kids."

"I don't want to share a birthday with the baby," Sofia said with an attitude.

Damian looked at his daughter and grinned. "We share everything in this family. Get used to it, princess."

She was old enough to understand our relationship with her mother.

"Gross, Daddy. I don't want to hear about that stuff."

Damian laughed. "How do you think you came into this world?"

Sofia shuddered, turning her head away from him. "Spare me the details, thanks."

One day, Sofia came home crying after school because a girl made fun of her for having four dads. Not like she broadcasted the fact to the world. But everyone in Devil's Creek had an opinion about our family. So Luca went to the girl's house with Damian. They had a conversation with her father. The girl's family moved out of town a week later. After that, no one ever talked shit to our kids again.

We drove home from the gallery and took the elevator to Alex's birthing suite.

She sat on the bed and breathed through her nose. "You would think after six kids, this would get easier."

Luca dropped to his knees on the floor and moved between her spread thighs. He put his hand on her stomach. "You can do this, Drea. Just like last time."

She clutched his wrist, giving him a seductive look, which I immediately recognized. For a few of her pregnancies, she was having such bad cramps we had to get her off to ease the pressure. I could tell what she was thinking.

So could my brothers.

Luca turned to look at the kids. "Ma needs to rest without everyone hovering over her." He removed his cell phone from his pocket, spoke to Adriana, and addressed the kids again. "Nonno and Adriana are waiting for you downstairs."

The twins and Sofia looked relieved they didn't have to hang out for the birth. Bastian handed Marcus to Sofia, and Eve grabbed Cato's hand. They left the room a minute later, and I locked the door behind them.

"You didn't have to kick the kids out," Alex said, even though she looked happy about his decision.

Luca shoved Alex's dress up and kissed the soft skin of her inner thigh. "Yes, I did. You need to cum. We can make you feel better." He pressed his hand to her stomach and guided her back to the bed. "Let us take care of our wife."

Damian got on the bed with her and kissed her pretty pink lips while Luca stripped off her panties and licked her clit. She hissed each time he sucked on her, fisting his black hair in her hand.

"Oh, God, Luca."

"That's it, baby girl." He licked her pussy. "Say my name. Cum all over my face."

I got on the floor beside Luca and tapped his arm. After years of learning how to navigate our relationship with Alex, we no longer had to communicate using words.

We switched places, and I split her down the center with my tongue, lapping her juices.

She moaned our names.

Bastian kissed her lips as he rubbed her nipple while Damian dragged his teeth across her neck and massaged her other breast. Luca planted kisses up and down her thigh. We found a good rhythm, kissing, licking, and sucking until she came on my tongue.

After the second orgasm, she groaned and put her hand on her belly. "Ow." She sat up with Damian and Bastian's help. "This baby is angry." Alex laughed. "I can't wait to get this little devil out of me."

"The doctor is on her way," Luca told her. "Just hang on, Drea."

"I think we have time. If this baby is like the others, we have at least five more hours of torture."

Bastian stripped off his tie and put it over her eyes. "Then I guess we better find something to do with the time."

Seven hours later, Alex delivered a beautiful, healthy boy. He had black hair and Alex's blue eyes.

Alex's gaze flicked between Luca, Damian, and me. "Well, one of you is the father."

Chapter Twenty-Four

LUCA

Four years later...

W e gathered in front of the house as the limo pulled up to the curb. The kids were on their way downstairs to say goodbye to the twins, giving us a few minutes to get our queen to act like one.

Alex was a mess, crying and clinging to my side. She clutched my silk handkerchief and sobbed.

Marcello was on her right, running his fingers down her arm to soothe her. "Do I need to kiss your tears away, princess?"

Bash pushed the blonde curls off her shoulder from behind and kissed her neck. "Relax, Cherry. The boys can handle initiation."

Damian was on her left and kissed her cheek. "Shhh, Pet. They're going to be fine. It's only a few months. We all went through it."

"A few months where they can't talk to their Ma." She dabbed at her eyes. "They need me."

I laughed. "Our boys are men now, Drea. They can handle themselves and don't need their mother wiping their asses anymore."

"Luca." She elbowed my arm, groaning. "Even after twenty years of marriage, you're still the same asshole."

"You wouldn't want me any other way." I winked, and she frowned, so I hooked my arm around her and kissed the top of her head. "You knew this day was coming, my queen. Angelo and Leo are Salvatores. They're adults, not babies. One of them will replace me on their twenty-fifth birthday, and they can't do that if they don't pass initiation."

She forced a smile.

Alex was mad at me, but she also wanted me to console her, tell her the twins would make it through initiation unharmed. There was no way they could endure the months of hell each of us had to go through to become Knights without it changing them. They had to bond with the other Knights through the process.

This was a necessary evil.

A brotherhood.

"I'm not ready, Luca." Tears slid down her cheeks. "They're still boys."

"Eighteen," I reminded her. "Same as my brothers and me. We all went through this. Even your brother. We're still breathing."

She bit her trembling lip. "I know, but…"

"The twins have been men for years. I taught them how to shoot when they were old enough to hold a gun. Marcello trained them in mixed martial arts. Damian showed them how to hunt. And Bash has been teaching them survival skills for years. They are more prepared than any of the acolytes."

Instead of handing the reins to Leo, who was older by three minutes, I wanted the twins to fight for the honor of becoming the Grand Master of The Devil's Knights.

They had to be strong.

Hardened by this life.

And they would work for it.

I pulled Alex into my arms and parted her pretty pink lips with my tongue. The quick kiss got her out of her head as she kissed me back.

When our lips separated, she stared at me, breathless. "I know what you're doing."

I grinned. "Is it working?"

She shook her head. "I'm so scared, Luca. After all the stories I've heard about initiation, I feel sick to my stomach."

"Baby, you're our queen. Do you need the crown to remind you of its strength? Of your strength."

She chuckled, blush dusting her pale cheeks. "No."

Alex only wore her crown on special occasions with the Knights. Sometimes, I brought it into the bedroom and made her wear the crown and nothing else. She was so fucking sexy. Seven kids changed her body, but for the better. Our wife had curves for days, her tits even fuller than before she had kids.

We were eighteen when we met, the same age as our twin boys. Back then, she was so young and naïve. Just as broken and damaged as the rest of us. But now, she was strong, a queen in her own right, and the one person who changed all of us.

After one twin succeeded me, Alex would no longer be the Queen of The Devil's Knights. And no one else would ever have the honor of holding that position. She was the only queen of our corrupt empire.

"Ma," Leo said as he walked out the front door beside Angelo. "Would ya stop crying already?" He wrapped his arms around Alex, towering over her. "No one died. Aliens haven't invaded the planet. It's not the end of the world. We'll be back at the end of the summer."

"And then, you'll be leaving me again for Harvard." She cupped his cheek and smiled. "I hate this."

"I love you, Ma." He bent down and kissed her cheek. "Stop worrying about us."

"Yeah, Ma." Angelo yanked his mother from his brother's

arms and patted her back. "We're grown-ass men. Would ya chill?" She raised an eyebrow at him, and he added, "Please?"

"So much like your fathers." She sighed, gripping their muscular biceps. "I'm going to miss both of you."

"We promise not to get ourselves killed," Leo joked.

"Not funny," Alex shot back.

I curled my arm around her. "Remember, I can see everything they're doing. Nothing is going to happen to them. I promise."

They would lie, cheat, kill, and steal. Do pretty much anything their Pledge Master forced them to do. But it was an environment I controlled.

Knowing I was right, she relaxed, letting her shoulders drop a few inches. "Give me one more kiss before you go."

"Ma," Leo grunted.

She raised her hand and beckoned him with her index finger. "Nope. Don't you Ma me. Get your cute butt over here and give me a proper goodbye."

The twins hugged Alex, smacking kisses on her cheeks. They were both six feet five inches and so strong. The twins looked like me, except Leo had Alex's blonde curly hair that he kept short. Angelo was my spitting image and even spiked his hair like mine.

I was so fucking proud of them.

They graduated with the highest honors from Astor Prep and would attend my alma mater, Harvard University, in the Fall. Soon they would be Knights. I couldn't wait until the day I got both of them on their knees in the temple, surrounded by the Knights, as I welcomed them into our organization.

This was tradition.

A rite of passage.

Their birthright.

My father and Adriana came outside a moment later with Eve. She was seventeen and going into her final year at Astor Prep. Cato went straight to Bastian's side like an obedient dog.

They had issues for years, but after Bash found some common ground with him, they were inseparable. He looked like Bash more each day and was fourteen, about to start high school.

Marcus clung to my dad's hip and was tall for a six-year-old. Adriana held Santino, who had just turned four. We knew the moment Alex delivered Saint that he wasn't Bash's kid. Alex wanted to name him Santino because he was our little saint. One more miracle after trying for a long time. We did one final paternity test and discovered he was Marcello's boy.

Sofia left for France a few days ago, where she studied culinary arts at Le Cordon Bleu in Paris.

She wanted to be a master chef.

None of us could cook, so she didn't get it from her parents. Damian taught her how to use a knife but left out how he acquired those skills. Eventually, she learned how to make pastries and entrees from our chefs.

As the twins were about to get into the limo, Willow Marshall's red Ferrari flew through the front gate and up the driveway. She hopped out of the car, dressed in skimpy black shorts and a low-cut red spaghetti strap top that showed off too much cleavage. Her dad wouldn't have been thrilled with this outfit.

The only daughter of Cole and Grace Marshall, Willow was best friends with the twins. My boys had a thing for the girl, even though they pretended their feelings were platonic.

"I'm sorry," Willow said in a singsong tone as she rushed over to my sons. "I got stuck in traffic." She flung herself into their arms. "You wouldn't have left without me. Would you?"

"No way," Leo said.

Angelo nodded.

My sons lifted her sandal-clad feet off the ground. She was a year younger than the twins and a foot shorter. And beautiful like her mother. Willow's parents both had blonde hair and blue eyes. But she looked like Grace's twin.

"Ma's already having a nervous breakdown," Leo said with laughter in his voice. "Don't give us shit, too."

"I'm not." She dried the tears sliding down her cheeks with her shirt. "But I'm going to miss you." Then she turned to look at Angelo and touched his cheek. "Maybe you, too."

Angelo snickered. "You better miss me, Willy."

Her nose scrunched at his nickname that he used to annoy her. "Just for that name alone, I'm going to miss Leo more."

Angelo bent down, whispering something I couldn't hear.

Blush spread across her cheeks. "Angelo." She giggled and slapped his chest. "Stop it."

Willow put her hands on her slim waist, shoving up her already short top. The twins' eyes lowered to take in each of her curves, looking like animals on the hunt and ready to attack.

I shook my head.

"They're so cute," Alex whispered. "Leave the boys alone."

I slipped my fingers between hers and squeezed her hand. "I didn't say anything."

"You didn't have to," she said with a groan. "I know what you're thinking."

In this case, she didn't know what trick I had up my sleeve. It was a thought that had been percolating for a long time. If our sons were to share one woman, it would have been Willow Marshall.

Keeping that in mind, I considered her a potential match. Our boys would have an arranged marriage. That was how we did things in our world. All of our kids would marry someone connected. And since Cole was a Founder and a Knight, Willow was a perfect choice.

The union was a smart play.

We could use the Marshalls' political connections. They were an old-money military family. Most of the Marshall men were either high-ranking military or politicians.

After everyone had said their goodbyes, I escorted my boys to the limo. I closed the door, so I could speak to them alone.

"Listen to me," I said in a firm tone. "You are never to tell your mother the truth about initiation."

"But she's the queen. Doesn't she know already?" Leo asked.

I shook my head. "No, and it will stay that way. She would be heartbroken if she knew what you're about to do to become Knights."

They stared at me with wide-eyed expressions.

"Do you understand me?"

"Yes, sir," they said in unison.

I wasn't lying to Alex.

It wouldn't help her state of mind to know all the horrible shit her boys would do over the next few months. Cato had a few more years until it was his turn. At least she had over a decade before she had to worry about Saint joining his brothers.

"I'm proud of you," I told them. "One of you will rule the Knights, and the other will become CEO of Salvatore Global. It's up to you to decide where you belong."

My father didn't give Marcello the same option, and he didn't want it.

"May the best twin win," Angelo quipped, always the smart ass.

"I'm the oldest," Leo said with an attitude. "It's my right to be the Grand Master."

I slid across the leather bench and held his gaze. "When I was competing with Marcello for your mother, I almost lost her and the right to become the Grand Master."

Leo's eyes widened. "Is that why Ma ended up with four husbands?"

The boys were old enough to understand all four of us fucked their mother. Leo often asked me questions as if he

160

were wondering what it would be like to share a woman with his brother.

A few times, I caught them with girls by the pool, in their rooms, and even in the garage on the side of the house. Alex didn't need to know about that either. It would have turned her stomach knowing the next generation of Salvatore men were like her husbands. I let her hang onto the idea they were still her babies.

I nodded. "So don't get cocky. Age doesn't matter. I will choose whoever is best suited for each position. Being the Grand Master is hard. So is being a CEO. You have to make tough decisions and do shit you won't want to do."

"Can we go to The Mansion when we get back?" Angelo smirked. "Ya know, to celebrate being Knights."

This fucking kid.

"Always thinking with your dick." I clutched his shoulder and nodded. "Sure. But don't tell your mother you've ever seen the inside of that place."

He laughed because that was the same thing I told him whenever he asked for shit that would have given Alex a stroke.

But they were men.

They weren't boys.

If they wanted to get their dicks wet by pros, who was I to stop them? My dad did the same shit with my brothers and me. All of us lost our virginity at the brothel—another Salvatore rite of passage.

"Dad," Leo said as I gripped the door handle.

I turned to look at him. "Yeah?"

"Any advice on how to get through the next few months?"

"Don't get yourselves killed. Your mother will be very upset."

"Dad," Angelo groaned beside his brother, who shook his head at me. "Seriously?"

I rubbed the top of his head, messing up his gelled spikes.

"Wanna know what Nonno told me before I left for initiation?"

They nodded.

I would never forget the advice my dad had given to Bastian, Damian, and me right before we left the same spot the summer after high school graduation. His words never left me because I knew one day I would tell my sons the same thing.

"You're a Salvatore. Make them fear the name I gave you."

"Love you, Dad." Angelo flashed a rare smile. "We won't disappoint the family."

Or you.

Or Nonno.

I could almost hear it in his voice. Angelo lived to please me but wasn't as affectionate as Leo. Kind of like his dad. I didn't show an ounce of emotion until Alex ripped it out of my cold, damaged heart.

I cupped each of their cheeks in my hands. "I love you both. But it will disappoint me if you don't come back to me with at least a few scratches."

I smirked, joking, but not really, and they laughed. Then I got out of the limo and joined the rest of the family. Everyone waved as the boys drove around the circular driveway, headed toward the front gate.

"They'll be okay," I promised.

Alex slipped her fingers between mine. "What did you say to them?"

I glanced over at my dad and tipped my head. "The same thing my father said to us over two decades ago."

It was time for a new era.

The next generation of Knights.

The Frost Society

Welcome to The Frost Society!

You have been chosen to join an elite secret society for readers who love dark romance books.

When you join The Frost Society, you will get instant access to all of my novels, bonus scenes, and digital content like new-release eBooks and serialized stories. You can also get discounts for my book and merch shop, exclusive book boxes, and so much more.

Learn more at JillianFrost.com

Also by Jillian Frost

Princes of Devil's Creek

Cruel Princes

Vicious Queen

Savage Knights

Battle King

Read the series

Boardwalk Mafia

Boardwalk Kings

Boardwalk Queen

Boardwalk Reign

Read the series

Devil's Creek Standalone Novels

The Darkest Prince

Wicked Union

Read the books

For a complete list of books, visit JillianFrost.com.

About the Author

Jillian Frost is a dark romance author who believes even the villain deserves a happily ever after. When she's not plotting all the ways to disrupt the lives of her characters, you can usually find Jillian by the pool, soaking up the Florida sunshine.

Learn more about Jillian's books at JillianFrost.com

Printed in Great Britain
by Amazon

24271109R00106